"May I help you?"

Rebecca Linden might be a school secretary, she might have eyes that radiated virtue, but her voice surely belonged in a bedroom. It curled around Logan's senses, made him think of dark nights. Long nights. Logan wondered how many teenage high school boys came back to visit their old alma mater in the hopes of hearing this lady twist her tongue around a few vowels. She could easily puree a man's mind just by muttering the phrase "May I help you?"—if that man wasn't on guard. Logan was all too aware of the lady's allure—and he was always on guard.

Could she help him?

She smiled up at him and he realized just how deep a violet her eyes were. Unusual. Mesmerizing.

Oh yes, she could help him.

The WEDDING AUCTION

The highest bidder wins...love!

Simon Says...Marry Me!—February 2000
At the Billionaire's Bidding—April 2000
Contractually His—June 2000

Dear Reader,

From the enchantment of first loves to the wonder of second chances, Silhouette Romance demonstrates the power of genuine emotion. This month we continue our yearlong twentieth anniversary celebration with another stellar lineup, including the return of beloved author Dixie Browning with *Cinderella's Midnight Kiss*.

Next, Raye Morgan delivers a charming marriage-of-convenience story about a secretary who is *Promoted—To Wife!* And Silhouette Romance begins a new theme-based promotion, AN OLDER MAN, which highlights stories featuring sophisticated older men who meet their matches in younger, inexperienced women. Our premiere title is *Professor and the Nanny* by reader favorite Phyllis Halldorson.

Bestselling author Judy Christenberry unveils her new miniseries, THE CIRCLE K SISTERS, in *Never Let You Go*. When a millionaire businessman wins an executive assistant at an auction, he discovers that he wants her to be *Contractually His*...forever. Don't miss this conclusion of Myrna Mackenzie's THE WEDDING AUCTION series. And in Karen Rose Smith's *Just the Husband She Chose*, a powerful attorney is reunited in a marriage meant to satisfy a will.

In coming months, look for new miniseries by some of your favorite authors. It's an exciting year for Silhouette Books, and we invite you to join the celebration!

Happy reading!

Mary-Theresa Hussey

Mary-Theresa Hussey
Senior Editor

Please address questions and book requests to:
Silhouette Reader Service
U.S.: 3010 Walden Ave., P.O. Box 1325, Buffalo, NY 14269
Canadian: P.O. Box 609, Fort Erie, Ont. L2A 5X3

CONTRACTUALLY
HIS

Myrna Mackenzie

Silhouette
ROMANCE™
Published by Silhouette Books
America's Publisher of Contemporary Romance

To my aunts—Mayoma, Bernice, Eloise and Willadean—avid readers as well as a very special group of ladies. Thank you for all your support and kind words.

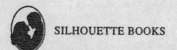

SILHOUETTE BOOKS

ISBN 0-373-19454-4

CONTRACTUALLY HIS

Copyright © 2000 by Myrna Topol

Visit Silhouette at www.eHarlequin.com

Printed in U.S.A.

Books by Myrna Mackenzie

Silhouette Romance

MYRNA MACKENZIE,

winner of the Holt Medallion honoring outstanding literary talent, has always been fascinated by the belief that within every man is a hero, inside every woman lives a heroine. She loves to write about ordinary people making extraordinary dreams come true. A former teacher, Myrna lives in the suburbs of Chicago with her husband—who was her high school sweetheart—and her two sons. She believes in love, laughter, music, vacations to the mountains, watching the stars, anything unattached to the words *physical fitness* and letting dustballs gather where they may. Readers can write to Myrna at P.O. Box 225, LaGrange, IL 60525-0225.

IT'S OUR 20th ANNIVERSARY!
We'll be celebrating all year,
Continuing with these fabulous titles,
On sale in June 2000.

Romance

#1450 Cinderella's Midnight Kiss
Dixie Browning

#1451 Promoted—To Wife!
Raye Morgan

AN OLDER MAN
#1452 Professor and the Nanny
Phyllis Halldorson

The Circle K Sisters
#1453 Never Let You Go
Judy Christenberry

The WEDDING AUCTION
#1454 Contractually His
Myrna Mackenzie

#1455 Just the Husband She Chose
Karen Rose Smith

Desire

MAN OF THE MONTH
#1297 Tough To Tame
Jackie Merritt

#1298 The Rancher and the Nanny
Caroline Cross

MATCHED IN MONTANA
#1299 The Cowboy Meets His Match
Meagan McKinney

#1300 Cheyenne Dad
Sheri WhiteFeather

The Baby Bank
#1301 The Baby Gift
Susan Crosby

#1302 The Determined Groom
Kate Little

Intimate Moments

#1009 The Wildes of Wyoming—Ace
Ruth Langan

#1010 The Best Man
Linda Turner

#1011 Beautiful Stranger
Ruth Wind

#1012 Her Secret Guardian
Sally Tyler Hayes

#1013 Undercover with the Enemy
Christine Michels

#1014 The Lawman's Last Stand
Vickie Taylor

Special Edition

#1327 The Baby Quilt
Christine Flynn

#1328 Irish Rebel
Nora Roberts

#1329 To a MacAllister Born
Joan Elliott Pickart

A Family Bond

#1330 A Man Apart
Ginna Gray

DESERT ROGUES

#1331 The Sheik's Secret Bride
Susan Mallery

#1332 The Price of Honor
Janis Reams Hudson

Chapter One

"Wow, would you look at all those women up there! All those—those legs and lips and skin and—and women."

The young man gesturing to his friend as they passed Logan Brewster's black Jaguar was looking toward the stage on the grassy area in front of the Eldora, Illinois, city hall. And no matter what his own problems were right then, Logan had to smile at the college-age kid's comments and rapt expression.

"Besides, the man definitely makes a very good point," Logan murmured, climbing from his car and heading for the center of the town where he'd chosen to locate his latest hotel. The Third Annual Summer-staff Labor Auction, scheduled to begin in just a few moments, appeared to be auctioning off only... women.

"Looks like it's your lucky day after all, Brewster," Logan whispered, even though luck had eluded him so far. He should have started his morning in bed with Allison Myer, his sometime lover and business associate, and then moved on to business.

The fact that he'd found a short, breezy note this morning—and no Allison—had changed everything, however. And here he was: assistantless and on the hunt for a woman.

Logan frowned at the thought. Allison's departure had been unexpected, to say the least. Lately she'd been hinting that she would be interested in a purely practical marriage. He'd been carefully considering her suggestion. A man who was incapable of love had no right entering into a union where he might wound a woman's heart or pride. But since Allison hadn't wanted love, and he'd considered her a friend as well as a lover and partner, a convenient marriage had made sense.

Waking to a note that indicated she'd left this town and him for a competitor had caught him off guard.

"But none of that matters now, Brewster," he muttered, glad he hadn't taken that irrevocable step toward marriage. "And you still need an assistant." Allison had volunteered to help him while his assistant was on an extended, much needed vacation. What's more, she'd known this hotel opening, his tenth, was more special than most and that the hotel's future manager's move to Eldora had been delayed by a minor medical crisis. And she'd still left him in the lurch.

So deal with it, buddy.

And he would. Quickly. For now he could manage without a wife, or a woman in his bed, but he needed an assistant for this job immediately. Finding someone for such a demanding role would be difficult.

But not impossible, Brewster. Nothing in business is impossible.

It never had been, not since the day he'd finally peeled himself off the street, climbed out of the alleys where he'd grown up and decided to concentrate all his efforts on courting success.

He'd done just that, and he was a lucky and contented man these days, Logan reminded himself, arriving at the auction site. Maybe this was an opportunity in disguise. Allison, for all her expertise, had disliked this midsized town's down-home atmosphere. He needed someone who could understand the benefits of both this town and his hotel if his grand opening was to be a success. This late, there wasn't time for one of his staffers to immerse herself in Eldora's culture. But a local lady would know this town intimately.

"Come on, already," one of the young men in front of him was saying, halting Logan's thoughts. "Would you stop talking about those ladies like you're trolling for a date? They're almost all teachers, man, at Alliota Junior High. Some of them were my *own* teachers. They could be my older sisters."

"Okay. You win. They're nice ladies, but…they're also babes," his friend insisted, turning to give him a grin.

Logan couldn't contain his low chuckle and the young man twisted around slightly to offer him a thumbs-up.

"Well, they *are* lookers, aren't they?" the boy asked.

"Absolutely beautiful," he agreed. And he meant that completely. These ladies were donating their time to help others. The thought of all that unfettered generosity in feminine form brought a reluctant smile to Logan's lips and his spirits lifted measurably. Today his plans and his business had taken a hit, but tomorrow was, well, tomorrow. Besides, the young man's exuberance was contagious, the sun was out, the grass was lushly green. And he, of course, had a job to do.

So do it. Make your choice, he ordered himself, taking a seat in one of the folding chairs set up on the grassy area in front of the stage. The auction was already beginning as he picked up a brochure someone had dropped. It listed all the participants and their background information. Plenty of ladies, and all he needed was one. The right one.

Logan sat back in his chair. No hurry. He watched the first lady begin her climb to the stage and immediately realized something extraordinary was happening before him.

A hush fell over the crowd, and Logan was pretty darn sure it had very little to do with the lure of the sale and everything to do with the woman on stage. The lady in question had long brown hair, shot with gold, that swept back as she glanced up toward her destination, but it was something more that made him take in a long, slow breath. Something that stirred the senses. An air. An aura. She moved gracefully with her head held high. Confident, Logan thought with a half smile as he shifted his long legs and lounged back in his chair.

"Look at her." He heard someone practically breathe the words. "Right off the meter, man."

Right off the meter, Logan silently agreed. And then he ceased to listen to the crowd around him at all.

At the top of the stairs the woman looked up. Her gaze met his, and he finally got a direct view of her. Delicately arched, sultry eyebrows warred with wide, slightly wary violet eyes, and Logan felt an electric surge race through him.

Out of place, pal, he told himself. He frowned at his body's reaction, mastered it, smiled at her.

For the briefest second, her lashes flickered, her steps faltered, but then she tilted her head and smiled back slightly, revealing a trace of dimples as she continued to move forward across the stage.

She was tall and slender. No hype, no jewelry, very little makeup, and yet she was arrestingly lovely. Innocence and elegance wedded into one package. A primly straight nose contrasted with temptingly full lips. Her red dress was simple, not figure hugging in the least, which only made it more wickedly intriguing, Logan decided. He also decided that he wasn't the only one noticing. There was a "struck suddenly stupid" look on at least half the faces of the men in the audience.

The lady didn't seem to notice. She turned her smile up a few watts. An innocent lamb among the lip-licking wolves, Logan couldn't help thinking.

"Good morning. Thank you so much for coming out on this fine June day," she said, her voice low and yet clear. She apparently wasn't afraid of the wolves.

"And thank you for coming out this morning, too, sweetheart," Logan whispered to himself, feeling a bit like a hungry wolf himself and absolutely irritated with his seeming inability to feel otherwise. This edgy mood must be the result of his unexpected change in plans. It would pass in time, but for now he'd tame his reactions.

"It's my honor and privilege to start things off today and to welcome all of you here," the lady was saying. "I'm Rebecca Linden, one of the organizers of this event along with Emily Alton and Caroline O'Donald whom you'll meet later. For those of you who think I look familiar, yes, I am the secretary over at Alliota Junior High, but today I'm here in a different capacity. Having won the coin toss, I get to handle the fun part of the auction. I get to announce the winner of the raffle for the motorcycle."

She said the word *motorcycle* so very properly, and yet her voice was so sensual that any man this side of dead would have sworn she was describing a sexual object, Logan mused. For half a heartbeat, he considered standing and asking her to say the word again, before he caught himself. That wasn't why he was here.

"You're definitely losing it today, Brewster," he muttered. His bad experience earlier in the day must have jostled his brains just a bit. Tomorrow he'd be completely recovered. Raising one brow, he settled back to watch the show.

"Of course we'll need someone to actually draw the ticket," she suggested, grinning at the waiting crowd. "I'll need a volunteer. Someone who hasn't entered the drawing."

Logan saw the young man who'd been so eager earlier snap his fingers in frustration.

She scanned the crowd. "Come on, now, you're much more reluctant than the children I work with. I really don't bite," she promised, studying her audience. Her attention centered on Logan. That mildly flustered look flashed in her eyes again before she checked it and moved on. Without stopping to think, Logan found himself rising to his feet.

"I believe I meet the requirements," he said, grinning as he slowly made his way to the stage. He only hoped she met his requirements as well. Now was as good a time as any to find out if they could work together.

He'd been told he could be intimidating when he was on the hunt. It must have been true because for a second the lady's smile nearly slipped away when he stopped at the edge of the stage right in front of her and looked up into her eyes, waiting. He wouldn't mount the stairs unless she said "yes," and he realized he wanted her to say it very badly, if only to hear her speak again. Of course, that was important. He'd read the brochure. Rebecca Linden seemed to be qualified to take Allison's place but the woman who ended up assisting him would spend a great deal of time talking. She needed to be able to stay calm in tense situations. She needed to soothe his customers. That, of course, was the only reason he wanted to hear the word *yes* fall from her lips. As for his impatience to move up the stairs and stand beside her, that tense eagerness so unlike him, was another thing. It was definitely out of place, and he intended to tame it.

But for now, he simply waited.

He could almost see her measuring the breaths she was taking, but then she recovered quickly. "You're sure you don't want to enter the drawing for the motorcycle?" she asked, gratifying him again with that word.

"He doesn't need a motorcycle. Drives a Jaguar," one of the young men called.

The sound coming from off the stage had her looking up, startled. Then she gazed down at Logan again. "Would you mind coming up here then, sir?" she asked, with a hesitant smile.

Logan slowly mounted the stairs, his eyes on the woman the whole way up and across the stage. She watched him approach, a bit nervously, he thought. When he reached her side and took her extended hand, her fingers were cold. They shook slightly in his grasp. He hoped she hadn't detected the slight current that had arced its way through him at her touch.

She looked down, and he could almost hear her taking a deep breath, but she immediately calmed herself. She gestured toward a sleek black-and-chrome number at the side of the stage. "This is our baby. It's a very impressive specimen, I've been told."

"It is that," he agreed. "Is this what Summerstaff raffles off as their grand prize every year?"

Her laugh was low and throaty, making him want to lean nearer. He resisted—because they were in front of a crowd, and because he always resisted when his emotions threatened to run away with him. It was how he'd survived, the way things had to be—for his own protection and for the protection of any woman unlucky enough to stir the flames a bit too high.

"We raffle off whatever anyone donates. The small items were raffled off in a ceremony last night, but the grand prize? One year it was a used car, two years ago it was a school bus, and last year it was a former police cruiser. The winner let me have a ride in the back seat." Her eyes twinkled at the thought.

Logan's own youthful years of avoiding the police were far enough behind him that he could enjoy her fascination with the subject. "Not your usual mode of transportation, I'd guess."

She grinned. "I drive a sensible midsize. And you're right. Guilt sits on my face like measles, so a criminal life would be a poor choice. No more rides in police cars for me."

A good thing to know, but then the news didn't surprise him in the least. It also wasn't exactly what he meant. A woman like her belonged in something more luxurious, swathed in silk and diamonds. If his luck changed today, he intended to supply the car, the clothes *and* the jewels for the next few weeks.

But she had turned to explain the rules of the drawing to the crowd. When she finished, she held out a basket to him. "All right. Make someone's dreams come true," she murmured.

For a second his eyes met hers and it was as if the stage fell away. She stared up at him and Logan could swear she wasn't breathing. He wasn't too sure whether air was sliding in and out of his own body, either, at that moment. The thought that he'd lost touch with reality, even for a second, sucker punched him, and he fought his body's reactions. Ruthlessly. So when the lady pushed the basket closer to him, he was able to manage a subdued smile. He did what he'd come up here to do—and made a young man in the audience very happy.

"Thank you," the lady on stage said, loudly enough for her words to be directed to the crowd, too. "Thank you for helping," Logan heard her say to him as he pulled the mask back over his thoughts and returned to his seat. When he looked up again, she was addressing the crowd.

"Once again, we appreciate your patronage of the Summerstaff Labor Auction," she said. "We just want to remind you that all the proceedings go directly to help disadvantaged children and their families. If you have questions, I'll be around for the duration of the proceedings. Please don't hesitate to ask for help. So now, I hope you'll join me in welcoming our wonderful auctioneer, Mr. Donald Painter."

As the applause grew, she kissed the aging man on the cheek and stepped away from the microphone.

"Thanks, Donnie," she said, her low, melodious voice still carrying the short distance to the rear of the seating area. "You're a sweetie for volunteering to do this for us again. Save a good job for me."

The warm, teasing tone with which she greeted the man wrapped around Logan's senses and he stopped speculating. The decision to acquire this woman was made instantly, the way he did most things most of the time. The slight, raw surge of arousal that slipped through him when she turned to leave the stage and looked up, her eyes bright with enthusiasm, rankled. The wolf in him was rising. He slapped it back down.

"You're way out of line, Brewster," he muttered. Because for all her exquisite, enticing looks, she was, he could tell, a hometown, born-for-traditional-love-and-marriage innocent. Red Riding Hood on her way to deliver cookies to grandma and spread goodwill to the world. Not the type he allowed himself to get involved with, ever. His strong, out-of-the-blue reaction to her was just a delayed knee-jerk response to his own suddenly single situation, a rarity for him these past few years. All he *really* wanted, after all, was this lady's services.

And so he waited until that slightly untamed urge to touch and taste was under control, until the lady had slipped away down the stairs. Taking his time, making himself wait, flipping through the literature regarding the auction, he eventually strolled toward the area behind the stage where she'd disappeared. A temporary workstation had been set up there on a makeshift wooden platform, and the lady in question was bent over a copy machine, which appeared to be emitting an ominous hum.

She studied it for a few seconds, pushed a few buttons, then finally bent over, giving him a delicious view of that gently rounded backside of hers and a lot more leg than he'd bet she was aware of. Running her hand over the side of the machine, she paused in one spot, drew her hand back and gave the machine a hefty slap with her palm. The humming stopped and she murmured a small, satisfied, "Yes, thank you!"

Logan couldn't help chuckling. "Ms. Linden?" he said, moving up behind her.

A slight gasp escaped her. She turned quickly, her hair swinging out around her in a warm golden-brown sweep, which she pushed away from her face. "Oh no, you didn't see that, did you?" she asked, and Logan found himself grinning against his will. The combination of elegant beauty and barely tamed candor that she exuded was…intriguing.

"See what?" he asked innocently.

She smiled back and raised her shoulders in a small, resigned shrug. "Well, we need a new copier at the school, but we're not going to get one, and so we just have to make do, which sometimes means being inventive. But I wouldn't want it broadcast that I regularly manhandle school property. And—forgive me. I'm sorry. You don't want to hear about my copier problems. You must have had a question. May I help you?''

The lady might be a school secretary, she might have eyes that radiated virtue, but her voice surely belonged in a bedroom. It curled around his senses, made him think of dark nights. Long nights. And touching. Lots of touching. Logan wondered how many teenage high school boys came back to visit their old alma mater in the hopes of hearing this lady twist her tongue around a few vowels. Dozens, he'd bet. Hundreds. She could easily puree a man's mind just by muttering the phrase ''May I help you?''—if that man wasn't on guard. Logan was all too aware of the lady's allure, but he was always on guard.

Could she help him?

''I believe you might be able to lend me a hand, Ms. Linden,'' he said carefully.

She smiled up at him and he realized just how deep a violet her eyes were. Unusual. Mesmerizing. Oh yes, she could most likely help him.

''You…have a question about Summerstaff or about how we operate? About one of the participants?''

''I have a question,'' he agreed. ''About you.''

He could almost see the moment she realized he wasn't going to be asking for anything ordinary. Her breathing deepened just a touch. Her hand pressed a bit harder against the cover of the machine she was leaning against.

''And your question is…?'' she prompted. He had to give her credit. She had the kind of looks that would have tempted men to hit on her on a regular basis, whether she wanted them to or not. And right now he knew he was studying her with a greater intensity than was polite. He was standing just a touch too close. But she maintained her cool. Good. She could handle stress. Not that he wanted to cause her any. He didn't want to bring that guarded look to her eyes again. Ever, if he could help it. He just needed to know that she could handle a bit of pressure. Now that he knew, he carefully stepped away.

"Allow me to finally introduce myself. I'm Logan Brewster," he offered. "I've been renovating the Eldora Oaks Hotel."

She let out a long, slow breath. Her smile became more natural.

"Oh yes, Mr. Brewster. I've heard of you."

Obviously that was a good thing. She apparently liked to know whom she was talking to. So did he.

"Then you know my business?"

"Who doesn't? You take dead or dying hotels and renovate them into luxury resorts, then sell them. They say that each one is a custom design."

He tilted his head in agreement. "Yes," he agreed, "and the Oaks is a milestone hotel." In more personal ways than he wanted to discuss now. "I'll want the opening to be special. I'm expecting a large number of guests."

She nodded, clearly not yet aware of where he was headed. "I'm sure it will be a beautiful grand opening. Even when it was falling down, it was an incredibly interesting building. I'd love to see what you've done there someday."

"How about today?" he offered.

Those violet eyes opened wide.

He held his hands up palm out and took another small step back, the way one might with an animal that was feeling slightly crowded. "In a professional sense, Ms. Linden, I assure you."

"A professional sense? You're looking for someone to work in your hotel then?"

He smiled at that. "In a way, yes."

She beamed back. "Oh well, then, you're probably looking for Gloria Angelis. She used to work the front desk at the Nightrider Inn during the summers when it was still open. Do you want to see the brochure that lists her qualifications?"

"I've read the brochure," he said softly. He knew the Summerstaff Labor Auction had been started by Rebecca and her teacher friends, Caroline O'Donald and Emily Alton, when a student of theirs had needed medical attention the parents couldn't afford. He knew the three women had recruited other teachers. He also knew that for three years, the proceeds of Summerstaff had gone to help needy children. And he knew he wasn't interested in Gloria Angelis. In any way. Rebecca Linden was the one he wanted.

Rebecca somehow maintained her smile. This man, this…Logan Brewster, was making her nervous. She'd noticed him when she'd been stepping onto the stage. Of course she had. Dressed all in black, he was beautiful. Tall, broad-shouldered, narrow-hipped, with dark hair laced with gold and commanding golden eyes that could make most women dissolve with desire dead in the middle of town with everyone watching. But then, she didn't want to be like most women, and hadn't wanted to for a long time. At least she didn't want any drowning, dangerous longings that could ruin a person's life. She shied away from real temptation, and she did it very successfully, too. Unfortunately, standing next to Logan Brewster, temptation was doing more than making an appearance. It was washing over her quite noticeably. In long, slow, body-beating waves.

Of course, that was to be expected. The man had been the topic of plenty of gossip the past few days since he'd been in town. He was reputed to be well versed in the art of satisfying women. He probably seduced women even when he didn't intend to.

At any rate, she knew just what to do to calm herself. She'd trained for this Olympic event a few years ago when she'd been in danger of doing something stupid and forgetting one of the cardinal rules of her life. It had been no problem then and it wouldn't be now. Just think cold, she told herself. Think ice, think polar bears if necessary, she added, steadying her thoughts and her reactions as best she could.

"If you need help at your hotel, Gloria would be your best bet," she offered, in that tone of voice she reserved for ten-year-old boys trying to decide if they should call home and tell their mothers they had to stay after school.

"You've had years of piano lessons?" he asked.

"A few," she conceded, her eyes widening, wondering where he was headed, but willing to let him lead—for now. He was, after all, a very rich potential customer, poised to donate money to the charity of her heart. If he wanted to ask questions, she supposed she would just let him.

"And you've studied ballet?"

"I'm not very good at it," she said carefully.

"But you're used to systematic instruction and

work that requires practice and dedication. And you spend your days greeting people?''

"Mostly little people.''

He smiled and her heart did a series of jumps before she managed to breathe in and out enough to quiet it down. "Little people are, I've heard, the most difficult to deal with," he said. His low voice thrummed through her body, as if he'd just suggested something indecent, which he hadn't. Then again, maybe she reacted that way because she'd *wanted* him to suggest something indecent. Which was not like her—and not true.

Think cold. Think cold, she reminded herself.

"I like little people," she answered. Her tone was defensive. She realized that. She couldn't seem to help it, given the unsettling thoughts rushing at her right now. But the man didn't seem to mind her tone. His smile deepened.

"I'm sorry. No little people at the Oaks, but I can pretty much guarantee you that some of my guests will behave like children from time to time.''

She opened her mouth to say something, to try to head him off at the pass.

"What is it you want, Mr. Logan?''

"Your help," he said simply. "I find myself unexpectedly in need of…help. Would you consider lending me a hand?''

Oh, he was so smooth. What woman wouldn't volunteer for the chance to say yes to this man when his voice was so sensual, his tone so earnest, those golden eyes so warm?

Not one. Almost any woman here would sacrifice ten summers and her sanity for the chance to give this man a hand—or more.

With that thought, the piercing howl of emergency sirens went off in Rebecca's head. She heeded them.

"I'll find someone special for you," she offered, reaching for the brochure. "What qualifications are you looking for? What's your job description?"

He took the brochure she was opening and removed it from her grasp.

"I'll be blunt. My personal assistant is out of town. The woman who was temporarily assisting me is no longer available, it seems," he said softly. "Allison was to play a crucial role in the opening ceremonies of the hotel. So..."

He held out his hands. "What can I say? It's a lot to ask, but I need a woman who knows the ins and outs of this town and can learn my business in less than two weeks. Someone who's used to greeting people, who can help me entertain a large group. Wealthy guests attending the opening ceremonies who sometimes act like small, spoiled boys and girls. I need a woman who can answer questions tirelessly. Someone who understands the discipline of training, is open to instruction and is willing to learn the feel of the building day and night. Someone who'll live in it and learn to think of it as a home for a short while, the way I'd like my guests to."

Rebecca looked up, even though her heart pounded faster when their gazes locked. That wasn't what she wanted. Pounding hearts and rushing breath and irrational thoughts had no place in her world. She liked her ordinary life with its safe boundaries. There was no way she could work with this man—or live in the same building with him.

"You want to transform me into your assistant to help you open your hotel?" The words seemed to slip from her lips without her permission. As if she was really considering his offer. And obviously she was. Probably because this cause *was* very important to her. This was something concrete she could do to help children. Accepting that, and the fact that this man had the ability to help as well, she sighed.

"That's what I'm saying, yes." He smiled slightly, as if he knew just what a struggle this was for her. As if he sympathized. Maybe he did. It was clear this wasn't the path he had originally thought he'd be following, either. His assistant was no longer available, he'd said. Rebecca wondered what had happened. A lover's quarrel, perhaps? And perhaps that was none of her business.

"And you'll train whomever you hire," she said, pressing on. "What will that entail?"

He studied her for long seconds. She looked up into his amber eyes. Trying to tell herself she hadn't even noticed the color of his eyes. Finally, he shrugged. "It won't entail anything simple, I'm afraid. Due to the limited time frame we have, training will be intense. It will involve immersion in many of the details of my business, in any formal social skills that are necessary, in cultural differences that may come into play. You'll need to absorb a working knowledge of the wine cellars, of fashion, of food, of the personal tastes of my prospective guests."

She raised her brows. "All that in less than two weeks?"

"Twelve days actually, with two weeks of events afterward. But I'll help you, Rebecca. I'm used to deadlines. This is doable."

She realized they'd gone from discussing her in the abstract to talking as if she were, indeed, going to do

this job. Maybe she would. Now that the facts had
been laid on the table, she couldn't ask any of her
friends to take on this daunting task. Not when she
was the one woman here who had some experience
of just what Logan Brewster was really asking for.
She knew how difficult and humiliating the process
of trying to transform a person from one kind of life
to another overnight could be. She'd had a bit of experience at that kind of unpleasantness years ago. The
kind of experience that had once changed her life in
all the wrong ways.

But that had been a long time ago. She'd been in
high school when her parents had died and left her to
the mercy of wealthy relatives who had found her all
wrong for their tastes. They'd tried to make her over,
dismissed her attempts to please, torn away everything she was and withheld affection until she'd gone
looking for it elsewhere. She'd gotten her heart tram-
pled almost immediately, and so when she'd found
James, who'd wanted her and married her, she'd
jumped. She'd loved him with a quiet affection only
to find out that she'd disappointed him just as much
as she'd disappointed her aunt and uncle. He'd desperately loved the woman he wanted her to be, but
she had never been that ideal woman, much as she'd
tried. Her inadequate affection had brought him sor-
row, and so, after his death in a skiing accident four
years ago, she'd made a promise. No more deep and
crippling emotions. No more trying to change herself
to suit others. She would never do that in her personal
life, but—

She looked up at the man waiting for an answer.

"You want someone malleable," she suggested.

"Someone who's willing to take an active part in the experience," he corrected.

"This *is* an auction, Mr. Brewster," she reminded him. "If someone should bid more for my services than you..."

"No one will," he promised her.

And no one outbid Logan's twenty-five thousand dollars for her time.

Chapter Two

Several hours after the auction and, after packing her clothes and bidding goodbye to her best friends and colleagues, Caroline and Emily, Rebecca was on her way to the Eldora Oaks in a sleek black Jaguar. It had been years since she'd ridden in such a car. She'd assumed that she never would again. But Logan had informed her that he had plenty of cars she could use at the Oaks. The right kind of cars, she assumed with a pang.

So it was starting. The attempted makeover of Rebecca Linden. Again. That feeling that who and what she was just wasn't…enough. Only this time she couldn't run. This time she had agreed and she had to stay.

She sighed, knowing that it wasn't Logan's fault. He had a job that needed filling, he had paid good money for her, and she had learned how to make the best of most situations she'd landed in for the past few years. Besides, this time she was an adult, and this was just a job, not her whole life. Those feathery feelings this man sent coursing through her were bound to pass once she and Logan had established an employer-employee relationship.

But at that moment, the man took his eyes off the road. He looked over at her, shaking his head slightly. "I'm sorry for rushing you off this way. It's pretty obvious that this wasn't what you wanted to spend your next few weeks doing, was it?"

She looked into those golden eyes, filled with concern, and felt her heart stumble. Oh, no. He had read her mind, and he was going to be nice. That was going to make things so much more difficult, make it so much harder to think of this man as merely her employer. Logan Brewster and his golden gaze were definitely going to make it much more challenging to think of these next few weeks as simply…work.

Rebecca's conclusion when she and Logan pulled up in front of the hotel was that the Eldora Oaks had been hit with a magic wand.

"Okay, Mr. Brewster," she said, gazing at the soft pink stone and dove-gray roofed cupolas of the building, which had once looked pathetic and sad and now looked…romantic. "You're good."

Logan raised one brow and smiled as he climbed from the car and walked around to open her door. "Logan," he said. "And I take it you approve of the results of the renovation?"

She gave him a patient smile as she stepped from the car and gazed around her at the softly scented gardens of pink and blue and yellow that surrounded the building, at the winding, tree-lined paths and benches that had not been here before. She tilted her head back and confronted the newfound majesty and grace of the building itself. "What's not to approve, Logan? It's been awhile since I've driven down this road, but I can assure you that the Eldora Oaks never looked like this before. I stayed here on my first night in town four years ago."

He grinned down at her. "Comfy?"

She grinned back. "If you like sleeping in a bed that sags in the middle. I spent all night clinging to the edge of the bed to keep from rolling into the man-made valley."

He raised his brows. "Sounds…entertaining."

"That's one way of looking at it, I suppose," she agreed. "At the time I thought it didn't bode well for the rest of Eldora, but I was wrong."

"You like this town, then?"

She nodded. "It's home, more home than I've ever had in my thirty-one years. And where's home for you, Logan?"

He shrugged, crossed his ankles and leaned back against the car. "Wherever I happen to be at the moment. Today it's Eldora, tomorrow somewhere else."

"And you like living like that?"

"I wouldn't live any other way, but I understand that my nomadic way of life isn't for everyone. Or so I've been told."

By women, she assumed. Women who wanted him. "Most of us do want a home and family," she said.

"By 'us,' you mean 'you,' I assume, and I apologize if you think I'm getting too personal, Rebecca, but when two people are going to work as closely as you and I are, and when our business entails acting as a unit, so to speak, it helps to know something about the other person's personality and goals."

"Fair enough," she agreed. "And yes, I do have goals. I want to complete my degree and become a school counselor. I also want a home and family."

"And love? Some of the men who'll be staying here will want the answer to that question, I can assure you. They always do." His gaze was intense, as if her answer was very important in some way. That intense gaze was making her nervous.

She swallowed and lifted her chin to look directly at him.

"I want love," she agreed, "but not in the way you probably mean. I've loved, I've been loved, I've been married. My husband passed away four years ago and although I hope to marry again one day, I think that love should be…comfortable. I'm certainly not interested in the type of intense emotion or passion that most people wish for."

She wasn't. Her own crashing path in search of acceptance had led to disaster in her marriage. James had been hurt by the fact that she hadn't been his ideal, his Cinderella, but a part of that had been because she hadn't loved him as deeply as he loved her. Long before she'd lost James on that snowy hill, she'd lost the gentle dreamer she'd married. To sadness. So she knew the dangers of strong emotions and now she steered clear of them. Affection was good and necessary as long as it was uncomplicated on both sides. No fire. No flame. No risk.

Logan gave her a smile warm as caramel. He held out both hands. "I'd be the last person to criticize you for choosing to sidestep the kind of heart-tripping love most people want. Especially since love in any form isn't on my personal to-do list. Some of us just aren't made that way."

"Exactly," Rebecca said, wondering why she didn't feel more relieved. Maybe because she'd already suspected that this man wasn't into love. And maybe because that smile of his was still making her feel as if shooting stars had invaded her body.

"So." She tried to think of something intelligent to say, something to make her stop wanting to lean close and get a good look at the color of his eyes. "Now that we know a bit about each other, why exactly did you choose me, Logan?"

"I'd think that would be obvious enough, Rebecca. You're composed, beautiful and you know how to work a crowd. It may sound shallow, but it doesn't hurt to have an intelligent, knowledgeable and lovely woman to help me charm my clients."

She took a deep and sudden breath. "Do you—that is, you don't expect me to—"

Logan swore under his breath. He tucked one finger beneath her chin, imprisoning her with a gentle touch, and stared into her eyes. "I don't expect that," he said firmly. "Not ever. This is strictly business, Rebecca. Between you and me, and between you and anyone else staying at the Oaks. It's all business, even if it's friendly. The terms of our contract will be very specific, and if anyone—*anyone*," he stressed, "should attempt to harm or coerce you in any way, he's out the door. Immediately. He's flat on his back in the dirt. I don't approve of men who take advantage of women, and the amount of money a man has in his pocket doesn't make his behavior more palatable. If I led you to expect anything other than that—"

Rebecca reached out as he released her. She placed a hand on his sleeve, felt the tense muscles in his forearm—and immediately pulled back from the warmth that seeped through to her fingers, pulsed through her skin. "You didn't. I just—well, these are different worlds we live in, Logan. I just wanted to be certain I understood."

His eyes darkened, narrowed. A frown grew, bunching his eyebrows together as he ran one hand over the tense line of his jaw. "Hell, I must be losing something, Rebecca. I'm thirty-four. Successful. Generally known to have a certain amount of finesse. But in the past twenty-four hours I've lost an assistant and now I've handled this so badly that you actually thought I might expect you to share yourself with my clients."

She frowned herself. "I didn't really think that." She hadn't. It was just that this man, well, heavens, it was difficult thinking straight standing this close to him.

But when she looked up, his gaze was fierce, laser bright. "What if I *had* asked that?" he said.

And because he was obviously concerned and upset, she was able to smile.

"Logan, I'm a school secretary. I spend a certain part of my day every day telling people 'no.'"

He shook his head in dismissal. "Those are children, not full-grown men intent on having their way."

Her smile grew. "Have you ever had to say no to an adorable blue-eyed urchin with crocodile tears in his eyes?"

Something that looked incredibly like pain flashed in Logan's eyes. "Children and I, well, we're just not a good match, so no, thank goodness, I haven't had that experience."

She nodded, satisfied she'd made her point. "Children and I, well, we're a very good match, but I can still tell you that there's no one more persuasive than a mischievous child who knows how to turn on the tears. Breaks my heart every time I have to tell them 'no, they can't have recess while they're on punishment,' and 'no, helping me staple papers doesn't erase the fact that they tried to forge their name on someone else's test.' I can be very nice most of the time, but deep down, I'm a hard-edged woman when I have to be, Logan. And if I'd thought you were asking me to sell my body, even for my favorite cause, I would have told you to take me home. I can't be tempted."

Logan nodded. He lifted his lips in a gentle smile and brought his hand back down to his side. "I'm very glad to hear that. But then, I knew you were special the minute I saw you. I was pretty sure you could handle anything that came your way."

His confidence touched her, but as they moved up the lane to the hotel, she couldn't help turning to him one more time.

"Why—why *did* your assistant leave?" she asked.

He halted immediately, a frown furrowing his brows. "Given the circumstances, that's a legitimate question, and I wish I could give you an answer, but I don't know the complete story and it's not my story to tell," he admitted. "Allison and I had known each other a long time. She'd volunteered to help me while my regular assistant was on vacation, so I don't think she left because I was a devil to work for. Regardless, I can guarantee that my circumstances with you will be different."

Rebecca knew in that moment that his assistant had been more than an assistant to him. She was pretty much certain that he'd been intimate with the lady.

Her breath shimmied. She needed to say something, do something to ease the rubber band–tight tension inside her.

"Thank you," she managed to say, "for reassuring me." And for telling her that circumstances between the two of them would not be like that. He'd promised things would be strictly business. And that was just what she wanted, too.

Most women might not be able to resist lying awake at night weaving wild fantasies about a man like Logan Brewster. But she could. She was safe from those reckless, intense and dangerous emotions that could ruin a person's life. She *was*.

Because she knew the risks she was facing here. Logan Brewster was a bold, seductive, tempting male; one who probably moved from woman to woman the way most men moved from season to season. He lived in a world she didn't fit into, and he didn't believe in even the warm, comfortable kind of love. That, combined with the fact that the man affected her ability to breathe normally, defined Logan as a risk she couldn't afford. But she'd learned the rule of know the enemy, avoid the enemy, so acknowledging that Logan ignited her nerves like supercharged Roman candles was a good thing. Now all she had to do was simply avoid letting those feelings have any power over her.

Instead she turned her attention to the building in front of her. She reached out to touch the sun-warmed brick, to admire her first sight of the interior as they neared the glass doors and she got her first glimpse of the interior.

Sunlight. Everywhere. Somehow he'd brought the

outside, the trees and flowers and light, right into the building.

"You must be a genius, Logan," she whispered. "This is spectacular. Impressive. It looks like a place a person would want to, well, to live." She ran her hand lightly over the curving, polished wood of one of a golden pair of benches located just outside the entrance. She felt the smoothness and the warmth of it, the glow it seemed to contain, and she looked up at the suddenly silent man beside her.

There was a touch of fire in his eyes.

"No question. I made the right choice when I chose you. Thank you," he said in a voice that was low and deep. There was something about the tone of his voice, about the genuine pleasure in his expression that made her catch her breath. She could almost envision him naked and warm, rising from a lady's bed and whispering those same words in that same tone.

With that thought, all reason fled her body. She obviously had to formulate a better plan for dealing with this man. Apparently thinking cold thoughts just wasn't enough. She had to try harder. But then the darn man took her hand in his. Her flesh met his flesh, heat spiking through her all the way down to her toes. And she knew that there was only one plan that would work in this minute.

Not touching Logan.

From now on, she'd remember that rule. She'd chant it night and day. But for now his palm was skimming against hers—and she did nothing to stop it from happening.

"Welcome to my home, Rebecca," Logan said. "Come on inside. I'll show you more."

Her pulse began to stutter. Wildly. This would be

a good time to turn and run back to her apartment on the other side of town, she thought. An excellent time to explain that she was the wrong woman for this job. Instead, she took a deep breath, squared her shoulders and stepped into the hotel, the home she'd share with Logan for the next few weeks.

"You're sure you want to get started on this now?" Logan asked, pulling up the files on his computer. "I know I told you that there was a great deal to be done, but I never meant to insist you begin working before tomorrow. You might want some time just to get used to the strange surroundings." And *he* might want some time away from this woman. His senses had been on alert ever since he'd first seen her, and he needed to give them a break. With good reason.

No one knew better than he the absolute necessity of control, the complete foolishness of giving in to rash urges, of allowing emotion to slip in and create problems. Untethered emotion had left his mother pregnant, penniless and alone on the streets after her lover and her family had deserted her. She hadn't cared for the son who'd cost her the world, but she'd taught him not to risk caring, and he'd learned—finally—after he'd gotten his own heart badly nicked one time too many.

But right now, the past wasn't what he needed to concentrate on. The lady causing him to think all these unwelcome thoughts was staring up at him, her chin resting in her palm as she sat several feet to his right.

"I'm sure if you just left me to figure everything out on my own, I'd be fine, Logan," she offered.

Maybe she would. It was clear from the information in the Summerstaff brochure and also by her manner that she was quite a capable woman, but...

"You can't always tell what a person's like by simply reading about them," he said, gesturing toward the screen. "Take our guest list here. If you simply looked at what's on the screen, you'd see that in twelve days we can expect a former politician, an attorney, several accountants and an up-and-coming film star. So what does that mean?"

Rebecca tilted her head, her eyes narrowed in thought. "They're obviously all professionals. They'll expect a certain level of service. And we'll provide it."

He couldn't help being pleased with her answer. It was so obvious that she'd been reluctant to come with him, and yet, here she was, determined to do what he'd asked of her. No complaining, no backpedaling, no excuses.

"We'll provide all the amenities a one-of-a-kind, luxury hotel should provide," he agreed.

"Personal service?"

"Absolutely."

"Which means knowing more than what the screen reveals," she concluded, gesturing to the black-and-white figures on the monitor. "So show me, Logan. Show me what I need to know."

Her answer nearly froze him for a second. He'd had other women say such things to him in almost that same tone of voice, but they'd been seasoned lovers of his and they'd been talking about...something completely different. Rebecca Linden was, he knew, speaking of nothing more than the business at hand, her thoughts and words had no underlying meaning, and yet, his mind was suddenly roving, imagining, tumbling images about his brain that he would be crazy to concentrate on. And so he didn't.

He attempted an easy smile.

"All right," he agreed. "Let's take the case of Brian Jaynes, the attorney. Wears Armani, stocks his garages with Porsches and Ferraris, knows his way around most major cities in the world. He's a man who's used to being treated well, so when he has business in Eldora, what's going to make his stay here different from any other night in any other hotel?"

Rebecca's violet eyes opened wide. She waited. "Better mattresses?" she asked, her grin revealing her dimples.

A chuckle escaped Logan's lips. "Definitely better mattresses, but also a personal touch. And by that, I mean a touch of home. Brian might be a member of the ruling class, so to speak, but he travels more than he'd like. And like all of us, he enjoys letting down his hair now and then. Brian happens to like sci-fi novels, big band music and playing the clarinet. When he's home, he also likes rice pudding with whipped cream. Comfort food. We'll make sure that he has the wherewithal to relax and indulge those whims while he stays with us."

She raised her brows, concentrating on him hard. "And how exactly do you indulge him, other than feeding him well?"

Logan shrugged. "We let him know we're here to see to his comfort. If there's a band playing in town, we provide him with tickets. If not, we equip his room with a supply of CDs, books and sheet music."

"And a clarinet?"

"If he wants one."

Her smile was wide and slow.

"What?" She had lifted her head for that smile. He was trying not to be dazzled by the tilt of her lips or ensnared by the desire to run his palm down the slender, curving lines of her neck.

"I was just wondering: when I stayed here four years ago, what do you think they would have said if I'd told them I wanted a clarinet?"

He grinned broadly. "Handed you the Yellow Pages?"

She shook her head in mock sadness. "Not even that. Someone had ripped them off the public telephone in the lobby."

"I'll make sure you have your own personal copy."

She blinked. "I'm—I'm not a guest."

The lady was blushing. Logan wondered why.

"And—"

"And you don't have to...indulge me, Logan."

But, oh, she made him want to. He'd almost been unaware that he wanted to until she'd said those words. And he wasn't talking about telephone books, either. He also wasn't talking about doing anything smart. He'd already made a dumb move this week, thinking that Allison could be a friend and mate as well as a business associate. He didn't intend to make a practice of making mistakes, and so he forced a deep breath of air into his lungs. He reached across the table to take the lady's hand in his own, forced himself to think of her skin beneath his as nothing special. He'd held women's hands before—many times. To coax, to soothe or simply to seal a business deal. The fact that this time he felt a tremor meant nothing. Except that he was aware that she was not completely at ease with him.

"Rebecca, for the next few weeks, we're partners. Business partners. And if I wanted to…indulge you, I certainly wouldn't do it with something as mundane as a telephone directory," he said with a chuckle.

She gave a low, shaky laugh in response, running a finger over the notes she'd taken. "All right," she agreed, with a little frown of concentration, "but if you try to satisfy every customer's fantasies, then don't people take advantage of you?"

Logan's hand tightened on her own and he let her go. The lady was concerned. About him.

He shook his head slowly. "Rebecca," he said, "I grew up on the streets of Chicago. Tough and fast and a fighter. If I'd stayed, I might have died there, too, but I didn't. I learned how to survive, how to stay one step ahead and how not to be taken advantage of."

Her gaze was earnest, interested. "How did you go from there to here?"

"Worked. Saved. Bought a little land, fixed it, sold it. Bought some more. In time I bought a fleabag motel and turned it into something, if not admirable, at least acceptable. And I learned how to get ahead by giving people what they couldn't get elsewhere. I know my business, lady. I live and breathe my business. And I never allow myself to be taken advantage of if I don't want to be."

She had been staring directly at him, but at his last words she looked down, lowering her lids. Like a woman just before she was about to be kissed. Logan couldn't stop the thought. Neither could he keep his gaze from dropping to her lips.

But just as he was swallowing hard, trying to keep a tight rein on his baser instincts, she opened her eyes wide, and he saw the lights dancing in them.

"Does that mean I still get my phone book?" she asked.

He rolled his eyes and shook his head. "It means we'd better get back to work before you tell me you'd like a ten piece symphony orchestra in your room. In the mood I'm in, I might just indulge you," he said with a laugh.

She shook her head back at him. "I don't think so. Not enough room in there for them and me, too."

"Your room doesn't suit you?"

Rebecca looked up into the man's dark amber eyes. Let-me-unbutton-your-blouse-slowly eyes. It was an effort to keep her heart beating in a steady rhythm, so intense were the sensations swimming through her.

"You know it's a beautiful suite with room for me and everything else I'll need while I'm here. So don't even think about trying to provide me with something better. I'm happy." And she was. Sort of. Logan had said everything he did dealt with business and that was what she wanted. The fact that the rest of her kept responding to him in a most unbusiness-like way wasn't his fault or his concern. And it wouldn't be hers either as soon as she got herself under control.

For the next hour, she concentrated on everything Logan told her, every word he said. When they were done, she could look at a photo and recite the person's name, occupation and a few details of that person's life.

"You're a natural hotelier," Logan told her.

But that wasn't exactly why she had such a way with names and faces. When she'd been married to

James, he'd liked for her to know all his business associates and she had done her best to memorize as much as she could. To hide the guilt of not loving her husband enough.

"School secretaries need to know the names of every child that passes their way," she explained. It was the truth. Her time with James had given her aching guilt but also this gift, which she was glad to be able to put to use in so many ways.

"I'm sure you're good at your job," was all he said, and she remembered his statement that he and children didn't do well together.

"Forgive me for asking, but...you've just donated a bundle of money to a children's charity and yet...you're not comfortable with kids?"

At his raised brows, she shrugged. "Sorry. In school, I spend a lot of time asking questions. It tends to carry over."

He shrugged. "Don't worry about it. That ability to draw people out is part of why I hired you. As for me, let's just say that I've seen way too many children who were merely the product of a swift, mindless mating. Kids who often broke under the stress or who grew up mean and wild and tended to make poor parents themselves. In my mind, licenses for parenting ought to be issued only to those who want the job badly and are suited for it. I'm definitely not."

Okay, he sounded very firm on that. She tried not to worry about how he'd arrived at that decision, but he'd obviously given the matter a great deal of thought—and he didn't really want to discuss it. She'd honor that, and she'd be grateful for the fact that their basic desires were different. No chance of ever falling for a man who didn't want babies.

"Fair enough," she said, patting the stack of papers in front of her. "No children, just hotels. And, if you don't mind answering one more question, why hotels? Why not...anything else? What brought you to this?" She held up her hands to indicate the roof over their head.

He smiled slowly. "Two reasons. One is that after I made up my mind to get out of the city streets, I wandered, I worked, and this hotel, this very one, was the first place I ever stopped for a night after I had earned enough to pay the price of a room. And the second is just as simple. When you've lived on the streets long enough, you don't take it for granted that you'll find a good place to stay every night. Hotels were a natural for me. I take my living space and my beds, especially the beds in this particular hotel, very seriously."

Rebecca couldn't look away from Logan. When he'd said the word "beds," she'd felt a bit faint. She had the feeling this man did, indeed, take his beds very seriously. And his choice of bed partners as well.

It was a good thing she wasn't going to find out any more about that. A very good thing.

"Speaking of beds," she finally managed to say. "I think I will go upstairs. To sleep," she clarified.

"To sleep," he agreed. "Sweet dreams, Rebecca."

As if that would be possible in a million years. Logan Brewster might have provided her with the best mattress in five counties, the most beautiful room she'd ever been in. Her room might have the best sound system, the most soothing music. It might be the safest room in any hotel she'd ever had the pleasure of staying at.

But if she got any sleep at all tonight, it would be

a miracle. Because Logan Brewster would be somewhere down the hall. And now she knew the man took his beds seriously.

That was a thought to keep a woman tossing and turning for at least four weeks.

Chapter Three

"All right, I'll admit it," Emily Alton said to Rebecca a few hours later. "I just don't feel comfortable having you roaming around an empty hotel with a man like Logan Brewster, Becky. The man is reputed to have a way with women."

Her friend's thoughts echoed Rebecca's too closely for her to be angry. And it was clear that Logan *did* have a way with women if her own reaction was any example. Still, she gripped the telephone receiver more tightly, determined that this conference call she'd set up with Emily and Caroline would have the desired result. They'd already discussed the man who'd purchased Emily at the auction—Simon Cantrell, a member of one of Eldora's oldest families. And they'd discussed the man Caroline had gone to—Gideon Tremayne, who was the grandson of a knight. Now it was her turn at bat, and Rebecca wanted to reassure her friends, not worry them.

"It's a very large hotel, Em," she said simply.

"Oh, that's good, Becky," Caroline said. "More beds to try out."

"Caroline..."

"Sorry, but I think Em is right. We want you safe."

"Logan won't hurt me."

"I'm sure he wouldn't mean to," Emily began, "but..."

"You know I'm immune."

"What about that guy two years ago? The one you nearly fell for who'd made it clear he was just passing through town."

"That's just it. I didn't fall. I resisted in spite of his efforts."

"He wasn't Logan Brewster."

It was the truth. The man two years earlier hadn't had half Logan's charm. She'd been interested enough to know she needed to keep her guard up, but then the only reason she'd been interested, she'd decided, was because she'd been sexually deprived. Of course, that wasn't something she wanted to remember at this moment, since she was now two years farther along the road of sexual deprivation. Rebecca raised her fingertips to her lips.

"You're not chewing your fingernails, are you, Rebecca?" Caroline asked. "If you are, I'll know something's wrong."

"Absolutely not." She wasn't. Not yet. And not for years. She wished she hadn't told her friends that little secret from her past. "Come on, now, Caroline. Emily. I want you two to stop worrying. Of the three of us, who has the most ice in her veins when ice is what's called for?"

Silence. Long, empty silence.

A squeaking sound like someone was about to say something and then more silence.

"All right, you win on that count," Emily finally said. "We've all got a healthy dose of control, but you are, in fact, the one most likely to keep her cool in a bad situation. But still, do you think it's wise to spend three weeks alone in a hotel with a man who consumes women like breakfast cereal?"

"Emily," Rebecca drawled. "Don't believe all the rumors you hear. I'm sure Logan isn't that voracious." Not that she was sure of any such thing, but…anything to help a friend past a bad moment. "Besides, we're not alone. There are cooks and gardeners and maids. My door has a lock on it. A double lock."

"Yes, but what if you're the one throwing open the door? The man *is* almost better than double-chocolate milk shakes," Caroline pointed out.

"I can be trusted to keep my door closed. Implicitly," Rebecca said sternly. "Believe me."

"Hmm. I know that tone, Em, don't you?" Caroline asked.

"Yep. That's the butt-out tone, and it only means one thing."

"I know. She really can be trusted. Sorry if we doubted your ability to resist temptation, but when that man came to pick you up at the apartment, he looked like the type who'd be comfortable with and without clothing," Caroline said. "We just had to make sure you didn't need our help. You know you'd never yell for assistance if we didn't force it on you."

She did. Her independence was a habit she'd picked up in the years she'd lived with her aunt and uncle, a result of the feeling that help wasn't available from any quarter.

Rebecca shook her head. No point in going down that road. She had learned from her past, she was happy with her life now.

"Becky?"

Emily's voice was soft. Worried again.

"I love you guys," Rebecca said. "Thanks for caring, but don't worry. I really do have everything under control. Logan and I have a business arrangement. That's all. When I got to my room there was a contract awaiting my perusal. I just signed it, and I can assure you that it was very explicit, very dry and very much nothing to worry about at all. Okay?"

"Okay. We won't push," her friend agreed. "And Becky?"

"Yes?"

"Now that we know you're all right, we just have to know one thing, don't we, Caroline?"

"Oh, yes," Caroline said, and Rebecca could almost hear the smile in her voice.

"What's that? Ask away."

"Well," Emily began. "We've heard—"

"That the tub in the bridal suite is ten feet wide, has pure gold trim, and a champagne fountain on the side."

"And there's a bed the size of Topeka, Kansas, with a never-ending supply of fresh rose petals in a Waterford crystal container on the nightstand. Is it true?" Emily asked.

"You're kidding."

"No," they both said, but she could tell from the laughter in their voices that they were.

"I'll check it out," she said with a laugh, "and report back, if you like."

"Do that," Caroline said. "And if you need anything, anything at all, we're just a phone call away, hon. Remember."

"I will," she said. "Plenty of phones around here."

Rebecca said goodbye to her friends and hung up, but after five minutes of sitting in the dark, she got up. Where in the world was the bridal suite anyway?

Night had fallen several hours earlier when Logan heard the almost imperceptible sound of footsteps padding by his room on the carpeted floor. The training of years long gone by clicked in instantaneously, and he rose to his feet, went to the door and listened again.

He grimaced at the thought that even many years after his ordeal on the streets, he still had hearing as acute as any other nocturnal animal. It had once been a means to survival. Now it was merely an annoyance. He knew his security system here was almost infallible. If there was someone wandering around the halls at night, it could be only one person. And he wasn't sure if his defenses were up to handling a late-evening encounter with the lady. His thoughts had been traveling to all the wrong places all day long. What paths would they wander at a time of night when any sane male would be thinking of a soft bed and an even softer woman?

A low groan left his body, and he tensed, forcing control on himself. The lady was alone in unfamiliar territory. It was a large hotel. She might be lost. Worried. She might be looking for assistance and have forgotten where his room was.

He unlatched the door and looked down the hall.

No sign of her. Damn.

He left his room, the crystal fixtures lighting his way down the long stretch of midnight-blue carpeting.

But the sound of her footsteps had stopped.

He continued, turned a corner—and caught the lady's mesmerizing honeysuckle scent. He was still six feet behind her when he finally cleared his throat to alert her to his presence.

She sucked in a deep breath, audible in the stillness.

"Logan."

"You're all right?" he asked, traveling the last few steps to stand beside her.

"Yes, I—oh bother," she said, pushing her hands up to frame a face that was turning pink even in the dim hallway light. "I was exploring. I couldn't sleep and my friends had asked a few questions about the bridal suite. I just thought I'd look."

He chuckled. "They heard the rumors, did they? About the rose petals?"

"I thought they made that up."

He shrugged. "Come on, I'll show you." He took her hand in his own.

Big mistake was his first thought, even though he didn't let her go. Her skin was more enticing than rose petals had ever been. And this was just her hand. She had other paler, softer parts he couldn't see and definitely couldn't touch.

He closed his eyes, opened them again, trying to dispel the image. "It's right here," he managed to say, turning a corner, fishing out the master key.

"I—" her hand jerked in his "—I didn't think about the key."

"I should have given you one." If he had, she would have gone in, looked and probably been back in her room by now. She wouldn't be here in his clutches, causing his gut to clench and his needs to rise. He had to show her the room quickly and then send her back behind safely closed doors.

"Here," he managed to say gently, pulling open the door, staying in the doorway as she brushed past him, the subtle, feminine scent of her sending an ache through his body. "Fantasyland for the newly wed."

She walked into the room a few steps beyond where he was standing and then just stopped, her head tilted back, her long hair swaying over her shoulder blades.

"Oh my," was her only reaction for long seconds and then she turned to face him. He looked into her eyes...and wished he hadn't. She was wearing that wide-eyed look of excitement again. He was beginning to realize what it was that the wolf had seen in the innocent. Something sweet, tasty...tantalizing.

"There really is a champagne fountain, isn't there?" she asked. "And a tub with gold fixtures and a—" She turned back to stare at the long sweep of the room.

"Well," she said, staring toward the bed. "It certainly is just as I was told. It's—it's very large, isn't it?"

He wanted to laugh—or maybe to moan. The bed, as she had said, was indeed very large. Large enough to tempt any man standing in the same room with a woman like Rebecca. Tempting even to a man who had determined not to be tempted.

"It's a honeymoon suite," he agreed. Which only conjured up visions of what people tended to do on their honeymoons. The bed, he was well aware, wasn't so large that it was out of proportion to the room, but here, alone in this building with this lady in this room, it practically called to him. *Move nearer, run your fingertips over those curves you've been itching to touch, fit her body against yours, take her...to bed.*

His lids drifted low. He very nearly took a step forward.

"Logan?" Her voice sounded just as calm as ever, if a trifle small, but her eyes...she didn't seem to have the knack of keeping her concerns out of her eyes.

He raised his head and with great effort got the manacles back on the forbidden images he'd called up. The smile he managed was, he hoped, nonchalant enough not to reveal what he'd been thinking and frighten her. He shrugged. "The bed in a bridal suite needs to be roomy," he said simply. "Shall we go?" He considered holding out his hand, but he knew it would be an error in judgment to touch her right now. His body was still churning with the visions that had swamped him only seconds ago.

She tilted her chin high. "Yes, I'm ready. It's a lovely room, Logan," she said firmly. That composure he'd admired so much had returned to her eyes. He was glad—and proud of her. In spite of the control he'd worked so hard to gain over the years, he knew he could be a bit overpowering to those not used to the fierceness that still dwelled within him at times.

"I'll walk you to your room." He stepped toward her.

"No," she said suddenly. "I mean, that's really not necessary, but..."

"Yes?"

She looked up into his eyes. "I'm sure you'll understand that it's a bit disconcerting sleeping in a strange place the first night. I wouldn't mind some reading material. Since there's so much information I need to bone up on, do you have anything that might help? Information on the hotel? Books?"

She had moved ahead of him, her hair swaying as she moved. His gaze dropped to the small of her back. So neat, so perfect a place for a man to place his hand. So very wrong for him to even think about doing such a thing. Endangering innocence by his own wildness. He couldn't do it.

"Books? I'm sure I can find something for you in the library. If you'd like me to take you there...?"

His voice had dropped at the thought of being alone with her in the dark, enclosed spaces between the shelves of the library, and she'd obviously picked up on it. Her steps faltered just slightly, but she shook her head.

"If you wouldn't mind, could you choose something for me and leave it outside my door? I trust you."

Logan sucked in a long breath. She trusted him. Mad words for a woman to say to him when he was feeling the way he was right now. He was going to have to teach the lady more than just the idiosyncrasies of his guests and how to choose a wine. She definitely needed to know something about how to handle a dangerous male on the move.

"I'll leave a book or two outside your door," he agreed.

And he would find one for himself as well. Might as well spend the night reading. There was no way he would be getting any sleep—or anything else, either, tonight.

When Rebecca stepped into the dining room the next morning, she wondered for a moment if Caroline and Emily hadn't been right about the dangers of spending too much time with a man like Logan. She had awakened thirty minutes ago in a tumble of books and tangled sheets after spending the night dreaming of Logan's voice swirling through her sleep. She'd rushed through a cold shower, and she'd thought she was prepared to face the man. Yet, here he was, rising from the breakfast table, long-limbed and powerful, gazing at her with those breath-robbing golden eyes and saying—

"Time's tripping away, love. We're going shopping for your wardrobe." His soft, slow, "come-lie-beneath-me" voice crept beneath her defenses, dissolving her mind in a terribly disconcerting way.

But she needed to be alert now, to simply do her job.

"You're going to buy me clothing." Rebecca couldn't keep the slight tremble from her voice. She'd done this before, a million years ago. Made herself a blank canvas for someone.

Logan smiled down at her gently. "Relax, Rebecca, it's just a simple little trip into town to—"

"I can't let you buy things for me."

He held out his hands palms up. "Part of the job, angel. We agreed, you'd help me out of a bind, I'd provide you with everything you needed to do that."

She bit her lip, opened her eyes wide and looked

up at him. "Yes, but you told me you'd teach me. You didn't say you'd dress me, too." She looked down at the simple navy skirt and white blouse that she was wearing, cognizant that once again, someone wanted to wave a wand over her and change her into someone she was not. Like her aunt and uncle. Like James.

But Logan was looking into her eyes and smiling wickedly. "It's a lovely outfit," he promised her. "Innocent, the very kind of thing that must drive your male co-workers wild with frustrated lust, but you're a woman who can wear many styles, Rebecca, and for the opening ceremonies, we're looking for something just a little different, something a bit more…"

"I know. Sophisticated," she said softly, pushing back a strand of her hair that had slipped forward onto her cheek. And she did know. She'd walked in here knowing what was expected of her. It was childish to feel hurt and wrong to be stubborn just because Logan was going to mold her to his vision of the perfect woman. It was just a job and, like many jobs, there was a dress code. She attempted a smile. "You're right, of course. This is a Brewster inn and all of your guests are looking for an image. So—let's go shopping, Logan." Taking a deep breath, she stepped forward.

She smiled up into Logan's eyes.

Logan, the sudden victim of that sunny smile, knew just how frustrated a male could feel. The lady clearly felt more than a bit uncomfortable allowing him to dress her like a paper doll and yet she'd made a bargain and she intended to stand by her word. Physical beauty and a strong and beautiful nature. It was a powerful combination, he was finding. Almost too tempting to resist.

But he did resist. This lady wasn't looking for a quick tumble to assuage her needs and his. She was looking for love, home, family, the ever-burning fire in the hearth. All things he had no need of, things he would never allow himself to ache for.

Keep it simple, Brewster. Very simple, he ordered himself. Like Allison and all the ladies who had come before her. If this lady was fire, so be it. He'd learned very young that fire burned, and how to stay clear of the flame.

And right now he needed to remember that. The lady was waiting.

"Let's go," he agreed, firmly taking Rebecca's hand and just as firmly shutting out the reaction he knew his body would immediately succumb to. Not so difficult. He could do this. As long as she didn't move. Or breathe. Or talk. Oh yeah, especially that. The lady's lips could drive the most well-intentioned man over the edge into pure, driving lust.

"Where are we going?" she asked in that cool, quiet, sexy voice.

His hand tightened almost imperceptibly. He fought his reaction. "Somewhere local, special, a bit out of the norm."

"Not my favorite department store, I take it?" Her cool tones were laced with humor and Logan allowed himself to relax a bit and enjoy the lady's presence.

"Angelique would no doubt be highly insulted if we even hinted that there was any resemblance between her one-of-a-kind boutique and a department store. But she'd forgive me," he said with a laugh. The lady in question *had* gotten her start working her way up behind the scenes of some of those same department stores. He'd met her in just such a place when they were both still struggling and he was on his way through town. He'd kept track of her progress through the years and he knew she was grateful to all the businesses and the people who had helped her. Still, right now she was working hard to project a unique image and Logan understood that all too well to chide her for her pretenses.

Apparently Rebecca understood something of that herself, because when they entered the shop, she didn't blink an eye when Angelique appeared, wearing wild, bright scarves, which suited her, and a merely passable French accent, which didn't. Instead Rebecca smiled in that charming way she had.

"Logan tells me you're going to make me look elegant," she confided.

"Logan?" Angelique scolded with a frown, ducking her chin to give him a piercing stare.

He shook his head. "I know what you're thinking, love. She already looks elegant. And you do," he told Rebecca. "I merely want Angelique to do justice to you, my dear."

Angelique's smile transformed her plain rounded face. "Now that's better, you big dolt."

Rebecca blinked and Logan let out a laugh. "Angelique loves me," he confided. "If she didn't insult me, I'd know I was on her blacklist."

"Absolutely, you sexy monster. Now come on, my dear," she said to Rebecca. "Let's get a measuring tape and chart your measurements."

Logan sucked in a deep breath. He raised one brow.

"And you stay here," Angelique ordered. "I don't want the lady squirming while you stare at her."

Rebecca had gone a delicious shade of pink. "I'm sure you didn't mean to come watch," she said apologetically.

Angelique howled with laughter. "Then you don't know this man. He can't be trusted with women. Even knowing what he is, they offer themselves to him like so many luscious desserts. If you think he doesn't take what is offered, you're a bigger innocent than you look."

Rebecca's eyes opened wider, but Logan didn't bother answering his friend's accusations. Even though they weren't true. He was most discriminating and careful about the women he spent time with. He didn't consort with innocents, even innocents who made him want to consign his rules to the devil, he reminded himself as the minutes passed and Rebecca finally emerged from the back room. She was clad in a body-kissing spaghetti-strapped sheath of ice-blue, short enough to showcase those delicious knees of hers. She was also clearly uncomfortable about something.

"You're a master, Angelique," he promised, and the lady in charge nodded her agreement.

"The blue is perfect with those magnificent eyes of hers, and this—" she reached up and took a long white dress off a display "—will be a treat with her hair."

"Oh, no," Rebecca murmured, gazing at the slim, clean lines of the gown, the high neck, the back that dipped low.

"Oh yes," he said, staring straight into her eyes. "You'll do it justice like no other woman could."

But her brows tilted down, the smoothness of her forehead marred by her frown. He held up one hand, gave Angelique a look. She nodded and faded into the back room.

"It's not too revealing, Rebecca," he reasoned.

"No. It's just too expensive. When you said I needed clothing, I—you can't spend this much money to dress me," she argued.

He reached out, closed his palms over the soft skin of her upper arms, staring down into her eyes.

A part of his consciousness urged him to slide his hands against her, just to feel the sensation of his skin against hers. He ignored it with an effort.

"The dress—it's just business, Rebecca. All business." And it was. Of course. He'd hired her for a reason. He was putting up with all this temptation for a reason. She would look right in his hotel. She would feel right in his hotel. She would lend the Oaks something special.

She opened her mouth. To protest, he assumed.

"Business," he stressed. "You and I have a contract to fulfill."

She closed her mouth. "It's awfully expensive business," she argued weakly.

He was glad to laugh. "I can afford to spend money. You're a good investment, lady. A very good investment, indeed."

She looked up into his eyes as if to decide if he was telling the truth. He stared resolutely back at her. Unblinking. Unflinching. He released his gentle hold on her.

"All right. Business," she agreed with a sigh. Then she shook her head, smiling widely. "If you want to spend your money to dress me and transform me into the perfect hostess, then I bow to your wishes, Mr. Brewster." She dropped him a sweeping curtsy. He found himself gazing at the top of her shiny hair, looking down into eyes turned suddenly elfin, getting more than a glimpse of the gentle swell of her breasts. "You and I will do business," she agreed.

From that moment on, Rebecca allowed Angelique to work her magic. The designer swathed her in silks, cloaked her in cream-colored linen and accessorized her to the hilt.

"And now," Angelique hinted, and Logan took his cue. He followed Angelique back to a small table.

"Just a few details, Rebecca," he whispered. "I'll be right there."

He watched as Rebecca busied herself in halfheartedly thumbing through the racks, watching the other customers that drifted in and out. As he spoke to Angelique and chose a few final necessary items, Logan noted a minor change in the atmosphere.

A small shriek, the strange rustling of a rack of clothing, a tiny hint of childlike sobbing. His chest felt suddenly tight and the room immeasurably smaller. He felt the need to get out of this small space and move out the door, but he stopped himself. He'd faced this before, a child's cry rolling back the years for him. His mother. Bitter. Angry. And in need of a target.

But he wasn't a target anymore, he reminded himself. And this wasn't the past. It was now, and now was very, very good.

"Oh dear, the poor child's mother is in the dressing room," Angelique was whispering as the little girl continued to whimper softly. "I'd better go find her and let her know that her baby is scared."

But even as she spoke, Logan saw Rebecca kneeling outside the circular rack of clothing.

"Don't cry, sweetheart," he heard her say. "Your mommy's just a few steps away. She hasn't left you alone, you know. And she wouldn't want you to be sad or worried. Soon, very soon, she'll be right back here with you. We'll watch for her together."

And Rebecca sank gracefully to the floor, her skirt swirling out about her. She placed herself at eye level with the little girl. She waited.

Slowly the golden-haired moppet peeked out, her eyes tear-streaked as she snuffled piteously. She took one look at the mahogany-haired Madonna smiling encouragement from a safe few feet away and the little girl ducked her head back behind a pink satin blouse.

"I won't come closer, love," Rebecca promised. "I'll just stay here until your mommy comes to find you. So that you'll be safe. Too many things in this room for a little girl like you to choke on or trip over."

She was right, Logan knew. Angelique's shop was a veritable treasure-house of earrings and pins, long strands of beads lying on small benches and tables. Racks with legs to trip the newly walking.

He knew that, because he knew this shop, not because he saw it right now. He didn't. He couldn't tear his eyes from Rebecca. She was sitting there in the emerald silk two-piece dress he'd insisted she wear out of the store and she looked like—her eyes were like two violet stars as she watched the child before her. It almost hurt to watch her as the child finally came out of hiding and gurgled a laugh at the beautiful lady watching over her. Rebecca Linden. She really was just what he'd proclaimed her to be, innocence, a woman who wanted a family above all else. A woman meant for a man who wanted the same things she wanted. She would have them. Obviously, some man, some perfect father type would come and deliver the full package to her someday.

"She's beautiful, isn't she?" Angelique whispered.

"Yes, of course," he agreed as the mother rushed from the dressing room and found her child, breaking the spell. "She'll be an—an asset to the Oaks. I chose well, didn't I?" he asked, as Rebecca rose to her feet and began to walk toward them on legs that were long and elegant and shaped to drive a man to dream wicked dreams.

Angelique wrinkled her brow and poked him in the arm. "An asset? Get real, Logan. You burn when you look at her."

He turned to his old friend. "It's business, Angelique." And if she was right, he would ignore that annoying little fact. He would bend the situation to his wishes, the way he always did. Rebecca Linden would be only another associate if he had to pack himself in ice five times a day.

He gazed at the lady in question as she reached his side. She was smiling, comfortable in a way she hadn't been when they first entered the shop. He wondered how much the child had to do with that.

"You charmed that little girl, Rebecca," Angelique said with bold approval, indicating the child who was happily waving her pudgy hands toward Rebecca now. "You should have babies. Lots of them."

Rebecca returned the other woman's smile although she glanced at Logan out of the corner of her eye and he was certain he detected a hint of tension there. "Thank you. I intend to. And also, thank you for being patient with me today. I'm afraid I'm not the most conformable customer," she admitted.

"Hey, what's a little resistance here and there? I knew Logan would talk you into doing the right thing. He can be very persuasive."

The smile almost seemed to freeze on Rebecca's face, but she quickly recovered. "You misunderstand, Angelique. Logan and I have a working relationship. This…all this," she said, referring to the bags and boxes stacked around her, "is strictly part of the job."

The other lady shrugged and smiled back. "Yes, business. Of course. And I'm very glad you're allowing him to…do business. He was right, you know. You're beautiful. I'll be extremely proud to have such a fine model wearing the designs I love to death. Even if it is just business, love."

Logan ignored Angelique's meaningful glance as she promised to send everything to the hotel and ushered them out of the store. Rebecca was right. Theirs was a working relationship.

And he had the very dry, very concise contract to prove it.

Chapter Four

"She thinks I'm going to sleep with you, doesn't she?"

They had walked only a few yards when Rebecca had made that announcement. She placed her hand on Logan's sleeve.

Logan placed his hand over hers. He stared down into her worried eyes.

"Angelique thinks the world revolves around clothing and love, but you and I have already discussed both of those issues, Rebecca. Haven't we?"

She continued to stare at him. Then her eyes lit up with relief. "We have, indeed. And what kind of woman would argue with a man who wants to dress her in gorgeous clothing and offer her room and board in a mouthwatering luxury hotel?"

Logan shook his head, let his eyelids drift low as he studied the woman before him. "Surely not you, Rebecca Linden."

She shook her head right back. "Not me, Logan

Brewster. I am, after all, the hotel owner's new assistant, and I *need* all those clothes to fulfill my contractual obligations, don't I?''

"Absolutely, love."

"And I certainly need to experience the Oaks intimately if I'm going to help the customers feel at home, don't I?"

"I couldn't agree with you more, you oh-so-perceptive woman, you."

"And if people think I'm sleeping with the owner just because he has a—a—"

"Bad reputation?"

She frowned. "Just because he's been known to be a connoisseur of women," she continued, "then I'll just have to demonstrate that our relationship is completely pragmatic and impersonal, won't I? I'll have to be the model employee, cool and calm and capable for all the world to see."

"No one is more qualified than you to do so," he agreed. "I knew it the minute I saw you."

She flashed him a smile of triumph. "Well then, Logan, let's start spreading the word. The Eldora Oaks will be opening soon and it is going to be a most professional operation."

He wasn't sure where she was going with this.

"You're suggesting…?"

She started walking toward the car.

"I'm suggesting that you take me to lunch. After trying on all those clothes, I'm absolutely famished. Oh, and Logan?" she said as he smiled and began to follow her.

He raised his brows. "Yes, Rebecca?"

"I think it would be a good idea if you started sharing all the little details pertaining to the Oaks with me. If I'm going to do this right, lead tours or converse with the guests or whatever it is I'm supposed to be doing, I'll want to know as much as I possibly can about the history of the building, the number of rooms, all the secrets that it holds. If I'm going to help you with your guests, I'll need to be a font of information. You'll need to help me fill in all the blanks.''

He did just that. They sat at a window table in the Heart of Heaven Restaurant and demonstrated to all of Eldora and the world that theirs was a truly professional relationship. Logan talked, Rebecca took notes. Rebecca asked questions, Logan provided the answers. And by the time they left the building, Rebecca had a much better handle on where the Oaks had been and where Logan wanted it to go.

She looked up into his eyes as he helped her into his car.

''There. I think we've definitely made a statement, don't you? Now no one will think what Angelique did. They'll know everything between you and me is simply business, won't they?''

Logan smiled down at her as he clicked the door shut.

''Undoubtedly. They'll know, Rebecca,'' he answered.

But his mind was careening like a tumbleweed in a sandstorm as he rounded the car. He'd sat there during lunch and watched Rebecca eat—and been enchanted by her enthusiasm for food. She'd leaned closer to ask him a question and he'd wanted to reach across the table, cup her face in his palms and devour the moistness of her lips.

If he had, everyone would know what *he* already

knew. The wolf had found Red Riding Hood wandering in the forest and now he was taking her home where he could have her alone.

For the first time in his life, Logan felt sorry for the wolf. Innocence was a lure more powerful than he'd ever imagined. He hadn't realized that before because he'd mostly stayed away from the virtuous doves of the world and because he'd never spent weeks alone in close quarters with someone as guileless as Rebecca. But now he would, and the truth was out. He respected this lady, he needed this lady, he wanted this lady, and it was going to be absolute hell keeping the chains on his desire for the next few weeks. He hoped he was up to the task. Touching Rebecca Linden could only lead to ecstasy, followed immediately by disaster.

Hours later, Rebecca knew why Logan needed an assistant. After poring over his computer files, she realized just what a large group of people were arriving for his grand opening. People he knew. People who'd read about him in magazines and wanted to be part of the show. Locals who wanted to experience a piece of town history and those who simply were looking for a night in a first-class hotel. The two-week opening would be laden with events. Definitely a two-person job. Minimum.

Moreover his files didn't just contain information on his guest list, but on his employees, past and present. She hadn't meant to look. She really hadn't, but when Allison's name had popped up on the file list, she just had to take a peek.

"Bad mistake, Linden," she whispered. The woman had been definite model material, born into a

good family, raised in the best schools. Bright, beautiful, sophisticated, Allison Myer had been a fitting
match for Logan Brewster in every way. She had been
the woman that Rebecca's aunt and uncle had wanted
to transform her into, the princess James had held in
his mind and loved to distraction, the woman she'd
resisted being.

And now she was going to stand in for such a
woman.

"Okay, deep breaths," Rebecca ordered, sitting on
the bed in her jeans, white blouse and bare feet. "You
can do this."

She *would* do this. This time she would allow herself to be transformed. Because Logan was paying her
for that very thing, because he needed her to be Allison's substitute and because she only had to mirror
the image for a short time. It was like holding your
breath underwater. Possible as long as it wasn't for
too long.

What was also possible, she kept reminding herself,
was keeping a safe emotional distance from Logan.
And no matter that he made a woman's pulse skip
erratically, a woman like her who got involved with
such a man was just asking for heart-slamming pain.
He was a man whose needs were very different from
her own, a man who knew what he wanted, and she
knew she wasn't on his forever wish list. Besides, she
didn't do mind-shattering emotions. The price was
just too high. And lust—well, lust and love were too
closely linked. If she was going to be very smart, then
she would also pull way back on the reins of any
potential passion that might arise.

"And Logan certainly makes a woman want to let
go of the reins," she admitted, sliding off the bed.

"But that's no problem for me. Won't happen. When these next few weeks are over, I'm going to begin thinking about finding the right man for me, one I can be comfortable with and who'll only want the simple pleasures of home and family. No mad rushes of desire. No intoxicating, frightening urges to run away to the woods with the man and tear his clothes off. Maybe I'll take another job when this is done. See if the auction had any employers still in need of someone for July and August. Who knows? I might meet Mr. Right. Everything will be fine. Calm. Manageable."

Her words reassured her. A bit, anyway. Now all she had to do was actually prove she really could stand in for the lady Logan had intended to have at his side. It was obvious that this hotel, his tenth, the one where everything had started for him, was very meaningful. She would do her best to be all he wanted her to be, to do her job well. And so she marched to the closet, chose a belted cream-colored dress with a deep V-neck and slipped it on. Then she placed a simple twisted gold chain around her neck and small gold hoops in her ears. She slipped on her shoes and clipped her hair low on her neck.

The woman who stared back in the mirror did look the part, she admitted. That too cool appearance had gotten her in trouble over the years. It was what had made her relatives think she was without feelings, that she wouldn't care if she heard them whispering that she was a disappointing girl who lacked class, that she needed to be brought up to snuff. It was what had made James think she was the perfect woman, the classic, idyllic love he'd been longing for all his life. It was also what had made men consider her a challenge at times and why she had been forced to shore up her defenses against them.

"But for now, you look the part. Now let's just see if you can carry through without any missteps," she told herself.

She located Logan outside in the gardens, where he'd said he would be waiting for her. His black suit and white shirt gave him a slightly austere look, but when he turned and smiled at her, his eyes were warm and appraising.

"You look lovely, Rebecca," he told her.

The heat of the summer air and the scent of the roses that surrounded them combined with the fierceness of the man's amber gaze, and she found herself struggling to remember that breathing was necessary for life. But she managed, just as she managed to find her smile.

"Thank you. I thought perhaps we could do some role-playing to help me recall something about each of the guests."

He tilted his head in acquiescence. "Is this how you memorize most of the students' names?"

She laughed at that, dropping out of character completely. "Some of them I remember because they've been sent to the office for doing something good—or bad. Some of them simply need to be remembered so badly that my heart goes out and it takes no effort at all. With some, though, you're right, I do have to practice remembering their faces and voices and names. It's always worth it. Children respond when they know that you care enough to pay attention to them."

But when she looked at Logan, his eyes had gone dark.

"I'm sure that they do," he said carefully. "And I'm sure that you make them feel very…necessary and important. It's what you do, who you are."

And he was a man who didn't feel comfortable discussing children. How could she have forgotten?

"Who I am right now is your assistant," she reminded both of them. "Where should we start?"

"Perhaps downstairs," he said quietly. "In the main rooms. I haven't shown you more than the dining area and the lobby."

And so she carefully placed her hand on his arm. She allowed him to lead her through a large, enticing sunroom filled with plants and cozy nooks to sit and talk with other guests. She followed him through the kitchens where he introduced her to the few people who had already taken up their positions.

"Hello, Jarvis," he said to the head chef. "I've brought you a treasure. She loves to eat," he confided.

Rebecca blushed, but she nodded her agreement. "I do, and everything I've been served here is wonderful," she admitted.

The man smiled back, but he shook his head. "Not good enough," he said. "You're beautiful, but not nearly as plump as you should be. I'll make you something special tomorrow, Ms. Linden."

"Rebecca," she corrected. "And please, you've already won my heart with that killer chocolate cake at dinner last night. If you went to any more trouble, I'd absolutely never stop eating." She grinned broadly at him.

The grizzled man's eyes brightened like the glowing end of a good cigar. "To cook for you will be a delight, Rebecca," he said, kissing his fingers. "To-morrow, my special crème brûlé."

"Oh, sweet and ever-so-wise lady," Logan said with a low laugh as they walked away. "You've just won Jarvis's heart forever. From now on he'll pull down the moon and stars and bake them for you if you only ask."

"You told him that I ate a lot," she accused with a laugh.

He shook his head and grinned. "Only that you appreciated his efforts. And he's right, anyway. You're built like a willow and it's a treat to watch you eat."

His voice whispered through her, and Rebecca fought not to begin taking deep breaths to calm herself. That would be too obvious. That would signal nervousness when she wasn't supposed to be feeling anything. She was supposed to be trying to imagine Logan as one of the many guests who would be arriving soon. The ones she needed to know more about.

"All right, let's pretend you're Gerald Vanna. I understand you enjoy playing pool, Mr. Vanna. And by a stroke of good fortune, we happen to have a very fine pool table here at the Oaks. Please. Allow me to show you to it."

"A fine pool table? Well, well, that's almost as good as a fine woman," Logan said, stepping into character and rubbing his chin. "A man would be an absolute fool to turn down an invitation like that, now wouldn't he? Lead on, Ms. Linden," he said, playing along. "Do *you* play?"

She smiled at him politely and with just a hint of encouragement. "Not often, but I have. Once or twice," she admitted. "You might need to refresh my memory just a little, to help me remember the rules. This way, please."

As they talked, they walked, and when they got to the game room, Logan pulled back the door for her. The smell of leather drifted to her as she moved into the room. The furnishings were crafted of hunter-green leather and warm dark wood. There were high-backed cushioned chairs and tables with fresh decks of cards at hand. A long curving bar in the corner stood furnished with lots of sparkling glassware. And, of course, there was a world-class pool table.

The room was large, but it felt friendly and cozy, and suddenly Rebecca was too aware that she and Logan were alone.

Still she smiled and stepped forward, choosing a cue.

"Shall we play, Mr. Vanna?"

Logan tilted up one brow, but then he smiled and followed her lead. "Are you sure it's been years, Ms. Linden?"

"A few," she admitted, "but not too many. You wouldn't want me to merely let you win, would you? Not when I hear you have a stellar reputation at the game."

Logan chuckled. "He does have a stellar reputation, Rebecca, but if you look at him that way, he's going to think that you're talking about something other than pool."

She blinked hard at that. "I—I certainly never meant—"

"I know you didn't," he said, cutting her off, "and any other man wouldn't read anything into your words, but Gerald Vanna has another reputation as well. It wasn't in my files, although it probably should be for the protection of my assistants. The man thinks he's candy for women.''

"Well, then, I'll just have to show him that I'm only interested in one game, won't I?" she asked, pushing back her shoulders proudly.

Picking up her cue, she took the first stroke. When the clutch of balls at the end of the table broke apart, two balls fell neatly into the pockets.

Logan watched her with intense interest. It was clear that his very proper, very elegant-looking lady had held a cue in her hand before. She had a talent for the game—and she enjoyed it. When she sank her ball, she forgot that she was supposed to be playing the part of a cool, polished lady and grinned broadly. Almost gloated. In the nicest of ways, of course.

He played, too. Competently. But mostly he watched her, with great enjoyment. Her intensity as she moved into the game was utterly charming.

When she finally sank the last ball, she plunked down her cue, leaning forward to wink at him. "My game, Mr. Vanna."

Her lips were curved upward. One strand of her hair had escaped from the gold clip that held it. She was glowing.

He couldn't help himself. He stepped forward slowly, curved one palm purposefully around the nape of her neck and lowered his lips to hers.

"Your game, Rebecca," he agreed. Then he covered her mouth with his own again. With more depth and heat this time. He slid his hand down the buttons of her spine, he fit her body to his own and tasted what he'd been wanting to taste since the moment he'd first seen her.

A gasp and then a soft sigh slipped from her, opening her mouth to his plundering lips, giving him more of what he wanted.

She leaned forward, her palms against his chest. Her body trembled and then she angled her lips to his, fitting herself closer until there was no space between them, no room for air or breath or reason.

He tasted, sliding his lips over hers. Nibbling. Nipping. Deepening the intensity of the embrace.

The table was there. He could lift her, take her there, have her and finally, truly, completely, slake this thirst. And—and yes, commit a crime against the lady, he admitted, freezing as fast as he'd ignited, gently loosening his hold on her, steadying her on her feet. He didn't get this involved, didn't leave women expecting what he didn't have to give. And he didn't do wide-eyed innocents, even those who played a mean game of pool and had bodies and faces that could incite docile men to riot.

It was a good thing, too. She was standing there. Nearly swaying. Gazing at him with stricken eyes, as if she were in shock, as if she'd never been kissed before.

He could see her fighting to find herself, to regain what he had taken from her in the past few seconds.

"Good thing you weren't Gerald Vanna," she said, managing a shaky smile.

"I'm not sure even Gerald wouldn't have behaved better than that. My apologies, Rebecca."

She shook her head weakly. "You were…congratulating me on my win," she said, trying to give him an out.

"I was pushing you, taking what hadn't been offered," he corrected her. "I don't, as a rule. And I won't. Not again."

She clenched her hands, held them locked to her waist as if that was all that was holding her together. "Maybe you and I shouldn't play pool together."

He raised one brow. "Maybe you and I shouldn't be anywhere within ten miles of each other, Rebecca. But we are, and there's no way around it. So I'll just...be more careful from now on."

"I will, too," she promised. "That should probably do the trick, don't you think? After all, nothing can happen if we don't want it to."

And that, he thought later, was exactly the problem. He *had* wanted something to happen. He still wanted something to happen. But he had wanted things to happen before in his life and he had submerged those impossible wishes. As a kid, wanting a mother who doled out hugs instead of slaps. A boy on the street wanting to form bonds, but realizing that he thrived best when those bonds were loose and when there was an open door nearby. It was time to call on the lessons of the ages and just learn how to do without some things. Like touching Rebecca. Like wanting Rebecca.

He could do it. It would just take a lot of effort, and he was willing to put forth that effort because the alternative, starting something with a woman who wanted the constricting ties of the American dream, was just not a possibility for a man like himself.

Chapter Five

The lady was a treasure—and she was making him crazy, Logan decided two days later. She was running full tilt, studying hotel management into the wee hours, trailing every employee he had in the effort to learn how things ran, going over the activity plans for the opening Allison had made. Every time he turned around, he saw her elegant little fanny moving here and there, her violet eyes opened wide in concentration. He heard the low, sweet sound of her voice asking questions as she charged into her tasks and turned chaos into order.

"You should be grateful, Brewster," he grumbled, shoving a hand through his thick mane.

He was. This hotel represented how far he'd come from the streets. This one above all had meaning. He'd wanted someone to dedicate herself just as Rebecca was doing. Her concern for the people who worked behind the scenes sent warmth burrowing through him. Her enthusiasm, when he knew damn

well she hadn't really wanted this job, practically
slayed him. With the opening only six days away and
the usual unexpected glitches arising right and left,
he should be strewing jewels at the lady's feet. Instead, what he was doing was staying far afield—as
much as possible—afraid he'd lose himself and touch
her again. What he was doing was worrying about her
a lot, grilling Jarvis on how well she was eating and
asking Pete, who ran the gym, if she was getting
enough downtime to relax and exercise.

He wasn't happy with what he was hearing. Rebecca was taking care of his hotel, but he apparently
wasn't taking care of her. Not in the way he intended
to. That was about to change. It was past time he took
care of a few things, took better care of the lady, in
spite of his personal problem with keeping his lips
away from her. As if to add an exclamation point to
that statement, Logan met a somewhat pale young
blond woman moving slowly down the hallway right
that minute. One of the maids who'd started work just
last week.

"Terry? Are you all right?"

She nodded, somewhat shakily. "I was just coming
to find you. I'm not feeling very well, Mr. Brewster.
I thought I'd be all right to work, but I was making
Ms. Linden's bed and I felt so dizzy that I thought
I'd faint. She made me lie down and told me that I
was going home." The woman looked a little skep-
tical. "I've only been here a few weeks. This isn't
the way I wanted to start."

Logan frowned. "If you're ill, you should be home
in bed. I'll have someone call your family and drive
you there. And don't worry about the work. It'll get
done. We'll fill in for today, and tomorrow I'll get

the agency in town to send over a sub. I'm sure Ms. Linden won't mind waiting for her room to be finished this morning.''

The woman looked even more queasy. ''That's just it, Mr. Brewster. She told me not to worry, that everything would be taken care of. I had this awful feeling that she was going to clean it herself. That wouldn't be right, Mr. Brewster. She shouldn't be doing my work.''

But it would be just like Rebecca to step in and do just that. Logan looked down at the anxious young woman's face and smiled reassuringly.

''Don't worry about anything, Terry. Just go home and get some rest. I'm going to call Dave to meet you at the front door with a car.''

He was also going to stop in and see what Rebecca was doing with herself today.

He found her minutes later, clad in tight little cutoff shorts and a ragged red T-shirt, running a feather duster over the dresser in her room. She was humming softly—something he'd noticed she did a great deal—and her perfect little bottom was moving to her homemade music as she swished the dust away. The door was open and the maid's cart stood outside.

He couldn't help chuckling when she stopped midtune and whirled around, a guilty look crawling into her eyes. She opened her mouth to speak.

He held up one hand. ''I already ran into Terry, but you didn't have to get quite this hands-on, Rebecca. I have other maids who would have gladly pitched in for her. I would have paid them for the extra labor. As a matter of fact, I still will. You are not going to do all of Terry's work.''

She shook the feather duster at him. ''I know that,''

she said guiltily, "but it just seemed so prima donna—
like to sit around waiting for someone to come clean
my room, knowing it was extra work for someone. I
just couldn't do it. I'm really perfectly fine with this,
you know. At home, I actually clean my own house,
Logan," she whispered, conspiratorially.

"I knew you were quite a woman," he agreed.
"You probably live for the pleasure of ferreting out
dust."

"Well, I do know one end of a feather duster from
the other," she said with a toss of her head. "And
sometimes, yes, I do enjoy it. Gives me time to
think."

"About what?"

His careless question obviously caught her off
guard. Her chin came up like a rocket. Her cheeks
flamed a delicious shade of pink. Logan could think
of a million things that could have caused her distress.
Perhaps she'd been remembering that kiss they'd
shared. It had certainly been haunting his own
thoughts at the most inconvenient times. Or she could
simply have been thinking about something that was
absolutely none of his business. An embarrassing moment in her past. Her most private wishes. Another
man taking her in his arms.

The thought came at him, left him struggling to
back away from it, left a boa constrictor tightness in
his chest.

If he were smart, he'd get out of this room right
this minute. But he couldn't be smart. He'd come here
to take Red Riding Hood away from her good deeds
for a while. And he was pretty sure that if he left the
lady here, he'd come back to find her polishing the

marble floor of the lobby. She definitely had that I-want-to-help look in her eyes.

"Come on," he said, holding out his hand.

Her violet eyes widened. She looked at his hand as if he might be considering reaching out to touch her, stroke her, reel her in and kiss her. He was considering all those things, but he was not going to do any of them.

"Not coming?" he managed to ask.

"Where?"

The tension in her voice was so clear that he couldn't keep from smiling. "I'm not leading you to my harem, Rebecca. At least not today. I have a slight problem. Seems my assistant isn't taking the required amount of time off from her job."

She narrowed her eyes. "I don't remember reading about any required time off in my contract."

He raised his brows, stared down his nose at her. "It's understood, a verbal thing."

She raised her brows back at him. "The hotel is opening in six days. I don't have time to play."

"Lady, you don't have time not to. It's a requirement."

She crossed her arms. "Not in writing."

"I could put it in writing."

A sense of panic entered her eyes. "Logan," she said, holding her hands out. "I don't know if I told you, but I'm a little…nervous about this grand opening. I'm a school secretary. I don't have an ounce of the kind of natural know-how and experience a woman should have to make this fly. Not that I won't try, mind you. Not that I'm not going to do every single thing I can to make your opening a success, including cleaning rooms in a pinch if that's what's needed, but I just—I *need* to work. I can't go dancing off in fields of flowers.''

She was nervous. She looked almost as exquisitely calm as ever, but her fingers had flown to her throat and there was strain in her musical voice, and he, who should have been helping her deal with all this, had been avoiding her just because he hadn't trusted his hands to behave. Well, no more. He damn well wasn't going to let her think she was alone in this again, no matter how hot his blasted hands got.

"Come on," he urged again. "You'll be perfect, Rebecca. You've worked wonders just in the time you've been here. Things are running as smoothly as they ever do this close to an opening. More so than usual. What's more, the staff is calm, they're happy, and it's all because of you. You're doing everything I've expected and more. So come on. Let's go. I'm taking you for a much needed time-out."

She frowned slightly. Her skin was turning rosy. She was trembling slightly. "You hired me to do a job, Logan," she said quietly. "Please, let me just do it. I need to keep busy." She turned and began swiping some more dust off a table.

Okay, so he wasn't going to be able to give her feet and her nerves a rest by ordering her off on a break. That would clearly just make her more nervous. If that was the case, then he would make an end run.

"All right," he agreed. "No time off. But I'm afraid I'm still going to have to drag you away from the hotel today. The pianist Allison had scheduled for the Friday concert had to cancel. I have an appointment in town with a Mr. Grady Barron to line up some new musical talent. I hadn't meant to ask this of you, but since you feel you need to stick to business, then I'm hoping you know something of the local performers.''

Even though this was a task he had planned on taking care of alone, he knew he couldn't leave her here. She'd work herself to death if he didn't watch her. He'd spend his whole afternoon calling back to check on her. He was beginning to be pathetic with his concern.

"Do you know any local performers?" he asked again while he waited.

She shook her head. "Not well, but I do know Grady."

He smiled, taking her hand. "So what are you waiting for?"

When he touched her, he could see the pulse at the base of her throat begin to flutter. And the urge to place his lips against her skin and slide them over that sweet fragile spot, to taste her, was an ache growing inside him.

With great difficulty, he ignored the ache. She managed a somewhat shaky smile that finally firmed out. She drew her hand away.

"I guess we'd better get going if we have work to do, then. Just let me finish here," she said, looking around the room.

"I'll help you make the bed," he offered, moving to the rumpled sheets.

"I can do it," she insisted, and he noted that the delectable pink had crawled into her skin again. He lowered his lids, ignoring her comment. Reaching onto the bed to smooth the indentations out of the bedding, he realized he was running his fingers over the very spot where the lady had lain the night before.

Her body had fit there…and this would be where the swell of her hips would have been…her breasts, the long length of her legs.

Logan looked straight into the lady's troubled eyes, just as she yanked the bedding up and over the place where he had been staring. He tore his thoughts away from the path they'd been roaming and tucked the blanket in around the mattress.

She raised one questioning brow.

"I make a point of learning all the jobs I hire people for. I've made my share of beds in my lifetime," he conceded.

She nodded tightly. "You told me you had a thing about beds."

He forced a chuckle, trying to break the tension. "We're just making the bed, not crawling into it, Rebecca. I'm not planning on tumbling you down onto the sheets, especially not with the door wide open."

Her color deepened, but she raised her eyes to his, lifted her lips deliberately. "Wouldn't that add a little sparkle to your hotel's reputation? You could advertise that you'd tried out your guests' beds in every way."

His laughter was less forced this time. "You're a wicked woman, Rebecca."

"And a neat one, too," she said, smoothing out the last wrinkle on the bedspread. She looked around the room.

"It'll be seen to, Rebecca," he promised. "Natalie will be well compensated. She's probably on her way right now," he hinted.

That was enough to widen the lady's eyes.

"I should change. You should go," she said. "If we're going to visit the music shop."

And if they didn't want to be caught gazing at each other over a bed by one of his other employees, Logan thought, knowing where Rebecca's mind had taken her.

"Ten minutes," he told her. "And if you go near that feather duster or the bathroom floor, I promise I'm coming back to carry you away. I didn't hire you to clean rooms, Rebecca. Even if you are experienced. Natalie needs this work. She can use the extra money. She has three children to feed."

Immediately he was sorry he had spoken. The lady looked absolutely crestfallen. She looked down at the bed. He knew just what she was thinking and with a careless flick of his wrist he threw back the covers.

"Okay, are you happy?" he asked. "You haven't taken food out of the mouths of small children."

"You're going to pay her for work you'd already done?" she asked incredulously.

"I'm going to go nuts if we don't change the subject, Rebecca," he declared. "Go change, love. Everything will be back to normal and on the right path by the time we get back. Both Natalie and Terry will be fine."

But as for himself, he was beginning to wonder. Rebecca Linden was messing with his sanity, his sleep and most definitely his libido. The wolf in him wanted her in the worst way. He craved her body, her beauty, her sweetness…and more. It was getting to be an unbearable ache. And that was just too damn bad because he wasn't going to have her. The lady was going to leave here just as untouched as she'd arrived.

Leaving Barron's Music Shoppe later, Rebecca had to admit she was glad that Logan had asked her along.

She wasn't fooled by the fact that he had parked several blocks from the shop, taken her on a long, relaxing stroll to admire the flowers in the park and then insisted that he needed to stop for a root beer float at the soda shop. He was coddling her, taking care of her the same way he was known to take care of all of his employees. She was aware that he'd been checking up on her, asking questions about her, making sure she wasn't killing herself with work, and she was grateful, for everything he was doing this day. But that wasn't the only reason why she was glad he'd insisted she come with him.

The real truth was that she loved the Oaks, but it was almost a fairy-tale setting. Inside its walls one got the feeling that almost anything might happen, that rules could be broken with no consequences, that a woman could get caught up in the whole dress-up fantasy she was being forced into. She could forget who and what she really was, and things would still be all right. But out here in the world, reality was smack in her face and she knew differently. She knew exactly who she was and would always be. She needed to do that, to keep her perspective where Logan was concerned. He was a wealthy man of the world, a man with many Allisons. Naturally sophisticated women who fit his life-style perfectly. Women who didn't need to be changed or trained. She knew that, but…standing next to that bed with him, she had certainly lost her perspective for a second. She'd wanted to feel his lips on her body again.

The thought made her shiver. She looked up at Logan, hoping he hadn't noticed.

"So let me get this straight," Logan was saying as

the bell on the shop rang behind them. "We came here to find a new pianist for opening day and we left with not only a pianist, but a harpist, a string quartet, a group of Irish step dancers, a troupe of Shakespearean performers and a bagpiper?"

Rebecca looked up at him, furrowing her brow. "Do you think I overdid it?"

Logan's grin was instantaneous. "Sweetheart, I think your idea to have performers scattered all over the grounds is a wonderful idea. You trust your Grady," he said, nodding toward the shop, "to vouch for everyone's abilities?"

"You don't? But I thought you had made an appointment with him."

He nodded down at her. "I did, because he was the best source I had available, but I trust you more. I know you better than I know the man."

And he barely knew her at all, Rebecca realized. She wondered how many people had flowed in and out of Logan's life over the years. He was a wealthy nomad, and she had the feeling he made a point of never allowing too many ties.

"Grady knows what he's talking about," she said solemnly. "He's devoted his life to music."

"You know him well then." And there was a slight edginess in his voice. Of course, he'd want proof of why she was so sure of Grady's expertise.

She shrugged. "I met him when the school needed a new piano for the music room. He caught me sneaking in to practice after-hours on an old upright the school has had forever." She'd been embarrassed. Her aunt had berated her for not having enough skill, but she still loved music. "You could say that Grady's my music mentor. I don't know that much, but he sometimes invites me to the shop for a cup of tea and then he lets me con him into letting me play this old baby grand he has in the back. I love it. He'll make sure we've got only the best, Logan."

But the man didn't respond right away. He was frowning slightly.

"What's wrong? I promise Grady does know what he's doing, Logan. Really."

He touched two fingers to her lips.

"Shh, love. Nothing's wrong. I have absolute faith in you and your Grady. I was just—Rebecca, why didn't you say you loved music that much? I know you sing. I've heard you in the halls, but you've never even touched the piano in the lobby. I assure you it's a fine instrument."

She opened her mouth to speak and felt his fingertips against her skin. Warmth, soul-deep want began to build inside her. Her nerves blossomed to full blooming life. When he pulled his hand away, she wanted to follow with her lips, beg him to never stop touching her. Instead she forced herself to hold still, let the feeling pass.

"That's a concert grand you have in the lobby in case you haven't noticed, Logan."

He tilted his head. "Yes, and, your problem with that would be…?"

"I goof around on the piano. I'm not laying hands on something that magnificent."

At her words, the thought of laying her hands on Logan's magnificent body sprang to mind. She stopped thinking for two whole seconds. Breathe in. Breathe out. Breathe in. Breathe out. Okay, she was fine. She tried a lopsided smile, especially since his own frown was deepening.

"The piano was meant to be played, Rebecca. I don't have that many concert pianists stopping by all that often. Please—do me the honor of putting it to use."

Okay, she could manage a frown herself.

He grinned, leaned close, his lips almost against her ear. "It'll relax you," he whispered, his warm breath wafting over her skin. "Give you time to think without having to steal the cleaning supplies from the maids."

She pulled back slightly, giving her best mock haughty look. "Your ears won't thank you for this, Brewster."

"You like to play?"

She blinked wide. "Yes." Her answer was a sibilant whisper.

"Then I've just amended your contract to include a required practice time every day. Who knows when I'll lose another musician and need a substitute?"

"Another something you're putting in my contract? Can you do that?"

He grinned wickedly. "I'm the boss and I don't think I'm committing any illegal acts."

He was wrong. The man's very smile was an illegal act.

"I'll practice," she agreed, "but I'm warning you, you'd better hope and pray that you never need me to perform." Then he'd know that she wasn't qualified. And, Rebecca realized, she didn't want to disappoint him. It was a bothersome thought. She took pride in her work and in doing a job well, but needing a man's approval of her as a woman just wasn't a part of her life anymore. And it was totally out of place in this situation.

"Thank you, Rebecca. And please don't look like I've just asked you to sit under the dentist's drill for me. I just want you to take some time to rest now and then. I don't intend to force you to play the piano."

Logan watched her. He was glad when the lady lost that trapped-between-the-lion-and-the-lake look. Damn him, he'd been trying to do something nice for her, to let her know that she was welcome to indulge herself if she wanted to. Instead, he'd had her squirming and looking more worried than a mother duck who's lost a duckling with that crack he'd made about her contract. Rebecca took her work seriously. Too seriously, and he should have remembered that.

"Let's get you lunch," he said. "Jarvis will have my head if you lose a pound."

Her smile returned. "Jarvis? I had the distinct impression that you'd been badgering the poor man to keep an eye on what I eat."

"Me?" He managed that look of horror and shock pretty well, he thought.

"You. Any particular reason you think I need to have my menus okayed?"

He held up both hands. "Just doing my job, Rebecca."

"You do this with all the employees?"

He solemnly shook his head. "Only the ones who don't know when to take a breather. The ones who eat standing."

"That was only one day. I was busy."

"Uh-uh," he said, taking her hand and pulling her down the street toward a restaurant. "You eat right from now on."

"I'm an adult, Logan. Or is this in my contract?"

He gave her a lethal look. "I shouldn't have badgered you about the contract. Even jokingly. And I'm aware you're an adult, Rebecca. Too aware," he said, allowing himself for once to look directly at the fullness of her lips to make his point. "I know you think the money I'm paying Summerstaff for your services entitles me to a twenty-four-hour-a-day employee, but you're wrong. You don't have to prove anything to me, love. You're doing a wonderful job. Just…take care of yourself. Please." He almost said "for me" but he bit the words off. He didn't want her doing this for him, but for her. "You need to take better care of yourself," he repeated.

Her smile brightened the whole downtown area. "You're so good to your employees, Logan."

He took a long breath to keep himself from pulling her close and touching his lips to that smile. "I can be better," he promised her, "if you'll sit when you eat. Jarvis was practically ready to walk out the door. Nobody eats his meals standing, he told me. Remember that, will you, Rebecca?"

She nodded slowly, her smile still tempting him.

"You're the boss," she whispered. "And a very good one, too. All the people who work for you consider themselves lucky. You watch out for them. In spite of the huge number of people it takes to run the hotel, you know every single person's name. You can even tell Jed and Evan apart although they have the same job and are almost shadows of each other. Some bosses wouldn't be that way."

A small frown creased his brow. "Some bosses are fools. It's not that great an accomplishment, Rebecca. Every person who works for me is unique, important, deserving of care and respect. And a man's or a woman's name is his or her identity. It matters. Tremendously. So, there'll be storms in the tropics before I'd call one of my employees 'boy' or 'kid' or 'hey, you.'"

And it would be a long, long time before he forgot the sudden look of concern that entered her eyes. Logan realized he'd made a mistake, revealed too much of himself, invited someone close in a way he never did. He'd forgotten this was a lady who would remember that he'd been raised on the streets, a woman who felt for small children, a woman who would worry about what he'd lived through and wonder why he felt so strongly about certain subjects. He needed to be more careful if he wanted to maintain the distance he needed. But the lady's shining eyes were lethal. Her softness had opened a crack in his armor. And now it was time to close that gap, to cool off, to retreat, to move things back onto a simpler plane.

He searched for a smile. "I'll take you to lunch before we go back to the Oaks," he said.

"Following Jarvis's orders?" she asked with a smile.

"Someone's got to look after you. You hardly stayed out at all when you went shopping with your friends and that was several days ago."

She shrugged. "Caroline was just in town because she'd decided her boss, Gideon, needed to be introduced to the delights of designer ice cream, and Emily was attempting to play tennis with Simon, the man who hired her. None of us had that much time. Things to do," she argued. "Really."

"Lunch," he said, gently placing his palm on the small of her back and directing her toward the nearest restaurant. "Really."

But nothing was to be that simple. Outside on the street, they ran into some of Rebecca's students, two boys maybe ten or eleven years old and a little girl too young even for preschool. They crowded close to her, and Logan automatically stepped back a few paces.

"Hey, Ms. Linden, is it really cool living in a hotel? My mom says you're lucky to be one of the first people to see what the Oaks really looks like."

Rebecca grinned at the dark-haired boy. "It's even better than cool, Kyle. There's an Olympic-sized pool and I get the whole thing to myself."

"Whoa, did you hear that, Mindy?" he said to the toddler who was hanging onto the other boy's hand. "A whole pool just for one person?"

He gazed up at Rebecca worshipfully. She knelt before the little golden-haired girl.

"And how are you, Mindy?"

The wide-eyed child automatically reached up to pluck at Rebecca's dangling necklace.

"Mindy, don't," said the tight-faced young blond boy standing slightly to the side.

But Rebecca was already shaking her head, her bright shimmering hair dancing about her.

"It's all right, Jack," she said quietly, gently touching the boy's arm and gazing down at the little girl with obvious pleasure. The lady's smile practically glowed, Logan noticed, as Rebecca picked up the child and cuddled her close.

"Your little sister just wants to look at my bangles. It's fine. Here, sweetheart," she said, smiling at the little girl who smiled right back and wrapped her chubby arms around Rebecca's neck.

Logan studied her. His pose was languid, but every

bone in his body felt suddenly strained to the breaking point. The lady was so obviously in her element, so glad to see these children. That thought brought back memories of other days, other boys who'd never had an adult look at them with such welcome.

But the adults he'd known hadn't been anything like Rebecca. She swayed as she spoke, rocking the child almost unconsciously, turning to the two boys now and then to include both of them.

She glanced back at Logan once and he knew she was going to try to include him or call him closer. It was only with difficulty that he stood his ground. He shook his head just enough for her to see but not enough to attract the children's attention.

Her nod to Logan was almost imperceptible. She gave him his space, turning away to look down at the young blond boy again.

"How are things, Jack?" she asked, her voice careful but filled with obvious affection.

"Good. Good," he said, opening and closing his hands over and over. "I'm going to summer school, you know. Lousy math grades."

"But you worked hard," she consoled, lowering the girl to the ground. "And Ms. Hartman showed me the drawings you did of the field trip to the science museum. They were beautiful illustrations, Jack."

The child's smile was rusty but bright, almost painful, Logan thought, backing away from his own reactions.

"I'll draw something for you," the boy promised Rebecca.

"I'd like that. I keep the picture of the puppy you

made for me in a frame near the front door so everyone can see it when they come in.''

"Not even on the refrigerator?'' His smile broadened slightly.

She winked at him. "Well, I have others there, too. You draw a lot, you know."

He grinned and for the first time seemed to relax, his bones loosening into the awkward lanky stance common to boys who were suddenly growing tall so fast that their muscles hadn't yet learned how to conduct themselves. Then the boy's eyes focussed on Logan. His brows drew together.

"Is he your boss?"

Logan stepped forward slightly. He and the child studied each other warily, as the other boy watched with sudden interest. Only Rebecca and the little girl were smiling.

"I'm Logan Brewster.'' Logan forced himself to move closer into the circle.

"He's a good man, Jack,'' Rebecca said quickly, softly, and Logan knew that the child didn't quite believe her.

"My dad says that you're rich and that rich guys think they can do anything they want to. Don't—just don't you be mean to her,'' the boy said, blurting out the words, though he looked as if he wanted to run. It was a feeling that Logan knew well, and it was all he could do simply to stand there looking at the child when the urge to turn and walk was so strong. But Rebecca was here. She clearly cared about this boy, and at the heart of him, Logan knew he couldn't really turn his back on a kid even if he wanted to.

"Jack,'' Rebecca started to admonish, but Logan stopped her with a slight movement of his hand.

"It would be foolish for me to mistreat her, wouldn't it?" Logan asked, choosing his words carefully. "Because then she might leave me and go work somewhere else. She's her own person. She could do that," he said simply.

The boy nodded slowly. "She could do that," he agreed. Then, as if satisfied, he took his sister's hand. "Come on, Mindy. Kyle. Gotta go," he said. "Things to do."

"Have fun in the pool, Ms. Linden," the other boy said, raising his brows in a way that Logan was pretty sure annoyed young girls like crazy and would probably someday drive them crazy in another way.

"Thanks, Kyle. And Jack? You'll bring me a drawing?"

"Something special," the child agreed. "I'll figure something out."

Together the three children ran down the street in the mad dashing way that only children feel free to run.

"Thank you," Rebecca said softly.

Logan's laugh was faint. "For what? Making a child think that you need protection from your employer?"

She shook her head. "No. I'm sure he didn't really think that. He was just mimicking the kind of speech that adults indulge in when they're not really thinking very carefully."

Logan took her hand even though he knew the danger in touching her anymore today. He had been barely holding the wolf in him at bay all morning and the lady was turning out to be even more of a Red Riding Hood than he'd thought. Too giving for her own good. Soft. Openly maternal to any passing child, even the ones who could eventually break her heart if things worked out wrong, he thought somewhat savagely. What's more, she was way too open to a man who had nothing to offer a woman like her.

Somehow he managed a smile. "Don't underestimate the boy, Rebecca."

"I don't," she insisted. "He's so smart and talented. He's just—"

Logan waited.

"He's way too serious. His parents are good people but very demanding. They're so caught up in their work and their financial struggles that they end up giving Jack a lot more responsibility than most kids his age have. And sometimes that interferes with his progress in school, which is how he and I got to know each other so well. He just has too many adult expectations in his life for someone so young."

"So your job is to help the kid smile."

"Maybe. And to help him be a kid sometimes. It's not a job, though. I just—"

"You're a natural mother," he said, for both her sake and his.

She blew out a breath and smiled sheepishly. "Okay, was I that transparent?"

"About wanting to bundle them all up and take them home? Just a little," he said, feeling the cloud finally begin to roll off him. After all, they both knew and understood the situation. Knowing that she was a woman who had to be a mother and that he never would choose that route should make it easier for him to keep his passion in check. He hoped.

She shrugged. "They get to me. Especially Jack. He tries so hard to be perfect. I don't think his parents want to make him feel inadequate. They just want him

to have a better life than they do, but that often trans-
lates into them wanting to change him, to remake him
into someone he fears he'll never be. I know something about that."

He watched her and waited. "Rebecca?"

She shrugged. "I lived with an aunt and uncle after
my parents died. They wanted a daughter, but they
also wanted a daughter who suited their tastes. I
didn't. And so they did their very best to transform
me."

The way he was doing. What he had hired her to
do, he realized. He'd asked her to change herself to
fit his mold. He wondered why she'd agreed to do
something she clearly felt uncomfortable doing.

"It's different this time. A little," she said, looking
directly at him as if she knew his thoughts. "This
time I'm older. It's a job, one that I know is very
temporary. And this time I'm old enough to have
made some decisions in my life. I know exactly who
I am and what I want," she said clearly.

And who and what she was was Rebecca Linden,
natural born mother. She was innocent, proud and
lovely. What's more, she was everything he couldn't
let himself get close enough to touch. From now on,
he was going to concentrate on what he'd been concentrating on for a long time. This opening, his career.
Those things were, after all, the only things that really
made a difference in his life. They were the things
that had once saved him and everything else was just
a distraction...and trouble.

Chapter Six

For days now, she'd been neurosing about the hotel's upcoming opening, worrying that things wouldn't go as well as planned, worrying that she wouldn't be able to be all she was expected to be. But tonight she had to admit that a good part of her worry was actually centered on the man who was the Oaks.

"Just a man, Rebecca," she told herself, but she knew that wasn't true. Logan was much more than that. He was a man who turned her insides to warm vanilla pudding. He had built an empire from nothing and yet he worried about his lowliest employee, he knew every name, he genuinely cared about the well-being of those who cooked his meals and made his bed and dusted his furniture. He was appallingly uncomfortable around children and yet he had done his best to reassure Jack this afternoon.

He was just a man and yet—not. Because he was the man who'd been fueling her restless energy lately, the root cause of her need to do well. She knew this tenth hotel meant a great deal to him and she wanted to be and do everything right to make this work for him. He was the cause of her heated dreams. The memory of his lips covering hers made her tremble even just sitting here alone.

All of this was foolishness, foolishness beyond belief. Because of course all those aching wants inside her would go unfulfilled. She wouldn't let her heart start yearning for a man who was so clearly wrong for her. Then she would be just like James, wanting the unattainable, letting her emotions get the best of her, letting a drowning kind of love ruin her life.

"So don't be like that, Linden," she told herself, climbing from her bed, slipping her feet into red slides and belting her poppy-red-and-gold kimono around her. "Logan may be one of a kind, one in a million, but he's not going to be your hero, so stop dreaming and get your head right back where it needs to be."

She would. She'd do something positive right now, call up Deb Lerringer, who kept the records of each Summerstaff auction, and see if any employers had gone away still looking. Deb was a night owl. She would still be up, even after ten o'clock. And, Rebecca thought, maybe if she concentrated on finding a job for July or August, something to look forward to after she was done here, she'd regain some perspective.

"And then maybe…a movie, Rebecca. If you're looking for a hero, let's make sure he's just the fictional variety."

She'd made her call, had a promise from Deb to check out the possibilities for future employment and was on her way to find her celluloid hero a short time later when she wandered down to the small theater that the hotel housed.

"Logan was probably right," she murmured. "You just needed to relax a bit. All a woman needs some nights is warm milk, a soft pillow and a good movie." That would help her banish those thoughts of Logan that kept pushing at her.

Finally, she'd found the simple solution.

It was well past midnight when Logan did a walk through of the hotel. It wasn't that he was worried the security in the hotel wasn't up to snuff, because the security at the Oaks was the best that could be had. No, it was more a matter of needing to know that all was right. To see that for himself. And because, after all, this was his home. For the time being.

Of course, tonight there was also that little matter of his not being able to sleep. No question why. He was beginning to let Rebecca Linden get to him in a way that was just not going to fly. He'd already been wrestling with the urge to touch her ninety times a day. Now there was the added allure of her dedication, her warmth, enthusiasm, whether she was beating the pants off a man at pool or simply setting out to hire a pianist and coming back with a complete ensemble of performers. She'd been hurt and humiliated as a child and was determined to protect the innocent from enduring that same fate. She was equally determined to make his grand opening a success. The lady was truly amazing, alluring, and she was driving him to roam his own hotel at night, looking for peace.

"As long as that's all you're looking for, Brewster, we're okay. Just stay off the lady's floor. Don't go

near her door, don't go near her smile. Definitely
don't go near those long legs and curves.''

Restraint was definitely what was needed. Yet,
she'd been pensive when they'd returned from that
outing. She'd taken care of a few loose ends regarding
information packets for local attractions she was arranging for his guests and then she'd quietly disappeared. She'd had Jarvis send her dinner to her room,
and she hadn't come down afterward.

He was worried. More than worried. He'd bullied
her today, dragged her out when she'd told him she
didn't want to go. Now she was hiding, and he was
feeling like he wanted to hit someone.

"Try starting with yourself, Brewster. You're the
guy who had no regard for the lady's wishes.'' Just
like her aunt and uncle, he couldn't help thinking. Just
like those rich guys her little buddy had talked about.
He'd be lucky if she didn't leave him just like he'd
told the kid. He knew she wouldn't. She had too much
integrity to quit in the middle of a job, but damn it,
she might be wanting to. And it was his fault. He
owed her an apology. He wanted to give it to her now.
March right upstairs, pull her into his arms and promise she could do whatever she wanted to and he
wouldn't fuss about it.

Instead, he was doing the right thing. He wasn't
barging into her room. He wasn't invading her floor.
He was roaming. It helped him sometimes when he
got restless. Tonight it wasn't helping. The urge to
touch her, to reassure himself that he hadn't hurt her
feelings or hurt her sense of fairness, was like a jag-
ged knife going through him.

"Keep walking, buddy," he told himself, moving
down the cushioned corridors downstairs. "Keep

moving." He would. He'd stay away from her for
both their sakes. He'd just make one more circuit of
the downstairs, maybe go for a swim to try to tire
himself out and then he'd—

A sliver of light caught Logan's attention. The door
to the small theater was closed, but obviously someone was inside. And not just anyone.

Rebecca.

Alone down here. Like him. Probably struggling
for sleep. He should leave her to her own private
methods for curing insomnia.

It definitely would be a mistake to go anywhere
near that door.

If he were a very smart man, and he'd been told
that he was, he would do an about-face right now and
go back to his own room.

But he'd just about used up all his resolve. She'd
come into his territory, into his lair, and the need to
see her was just too great to withstand at least checking to make sure she was all right. Logan stepped to
the door, gently turned the knob and slipped inside.

She was crying. Long, trembling tears, a box of
tissues at her elbow, her damp hair falling over her
even damper eyes. Clutching a pillow and wrapped
in a fiery red robe, she sniffled, the tears sliding down
her cheeks in narrow, glistening tracks.

"Rebecca, sweetheart," Logan said, crossing the
room in three long strides and sitting beside her. He
reached out and lifted her onto his lap, wrapping his
arms around her and pulling her as close as he could
get her.

"What is it, angel? Has someone hurt you? Have
I hurt you?" He rocked her as he spoke, gently brush-

ing his hand over her hair, trying to soothe her with his body.

"Rebecca?" he finally said, when she still hadn't spoken. He pulled back from her just a touch so that he could look into her eyes.

Another tear took a long slide down her face and trembled on her chin before plunging to fall upon the back of his hand.

Gently he raised one hand to wipe the tears from her face, but she clutched his wrist. She stared back at him, her eyes big and violet and…flustered?

"Logan, I—I'm so sorry," she said, her words a bit choked, her eyes even wider, if that were possible. She swiped away the dampness on her cheeks with the backs of her hands.

"Aw, Rebecca, don't be sorry. I was the idiot who sent you into hiding. I should be put in jail for dragging you around today. I made you feel uncomfortable, and that wasn't my intent. You know I'd never want to do that."

She closed her eyes, leaning forward and hiding her face against his chest. "You're such a good man, Logan," she said, her voice coming out somewhat muffled.

"The hell I am. I ordered you around today. It was only because I was worried about you, Rebecca. I promise," he said, pulling back a bit so that he could see her.

Her lovely face had turned a delicious shade of pink. She was clutching the front of his shirt.

"You don't understand. I—oh, I'm so embarrassed."

"Because you were crying in front of me, sweetheart? Don't be. I'm not. Just tell me what the problem is. Is it me? Is it that Grady Barron? Did someone else hurt you today, say something to you, disappoint you? Just tell me, angel. I'll do my best to fix it.''

She closed her eyes then, letting out a little sigh that slid through his body and made him ache to pull her closer. But he didn't. He couldn't. Not now when all he wanted to do was to right whatever wrong had befallen her, undo whatever he'd done to her.

Rebecca took a deep breath. She opened her eyes and bit down on her lip gently, reaching up to swipe one hand over her wet cheek again, staring directly into his eyes.

"It's very hard to say this." Her voice was barely a whisper. He had to lean close to hear her words, and her lips…ah, he wasn't going to think about her lips now. Had no business thinking about anything but helping her.

"It'll be fine. Just tell me," he whispered back, and he ducked his head to brush his own lips over her damp fingertips.

"You say that because you're thinking I was in real pain, but—it was the movie, Logan."

He froze, his palms splayed on her back.

"Excuse me?"

She lifted one delicate shoulder, looked up at him from beneath lowered lids. "I'm sorry. Very sorry. I don't want you to feel self-conscious, but I was just crying, because—the movie was so sad."

With that, Logan did pull her close. He hid his lips against her hair, so that she couldn't see his smile.

"Are you—feeling a bit miffed, Logan?" she asked. "I'm sure I could have somehow managed to tell you sooner, before you—"

"Went crazy on you?" he asked, and he let out the chuckle he'd been holding back.

"You don't mind that I sobbed all over your shirt and got you all wet over a movie?"

He tucked one finger beneath her chin and tilted her face up to his.

"Was it a really good movie?" he asked, his voice low as he tried not to allow too much of his glee to show. She was obviously a bit sheepish over the incident already.

She nodded slowly. "An old one. Black and white. And the hero dies in the end. Tragically. I love it," she confessed.

Then Logan was holding her away, grinning at her before he let out a full-fledged laugh.

She stiffened in his arms. "It was a really sad movie, Logan Brewster," she insisted. "If you'd seen it—"

"I wish I had. You watch old sad movies a lot?"

She nodded a tight, sorrowful little nod. "It's this weakness I have. Do you know what I mean?"

"Definitely." He knew exactly what she meant. Unfortunately *she* seemed to be his worst weakness, but at the moment Logan didn't care. He'd been so worried that he'd somehow hurt her that it was pure relief to find she'd simply been indulging an affection for old cinema.

He chuckled again.

"Well, it wasn't *that* funny," she said, crossing her arms and trying to look angry.

"You don't think it was funny that I came storming in here determined to sew up your wounds and administer psychotherapy and chicken soup when you were only watching a movie?"

She raised her brows and the smile that he'd been missing made its way back to her lips.

"You were very...impressive, Logan," she consoled. "If I *had* been in trouble, you would have been just what the doctor ordered."

"Instead, I simply interrupted your movie," he said.

"Oh, no, it was already over. I was just recovering."

"You seem...fine now," he said in a suddenly husky whisper. She did. She seemed very fine, very warm, and he was incredibly aware of the softness of her breasts beneath the thin red silky thing she was wearing.

"I am," she said and her breath was warm and minty on his face.

The room seemed suddenly smaller than it was. The air seemed suddenly heavy.

"Rebecca?"

"Yes?"

"I'm sorry, but I'm going to kiss you now. If you're going to run, run fast."

She should do that, but she'd been wanting him to touch her again for days. She needed just a small taste of him to take the edge off her wanting.

She slid her fingers into his hair, angled her face so that his mouth could meet hers more easily and melted beneath him.

Rebecca knew she was playing with crazy cards. No way of winning in the long run, but the need to feel the crush of Logan's mouth against her own, the tightening of his arms about her was an insistent tug-of-war with her will. For just this moment, she would stop tugging and give in, let go, just feel.

She craved his touch. If she was going to get him out of her bloodstream, then she darn well needed to let those skillful lips have their way as she leaned her head back and he nuzzled a path down her neck, lingering on the dip in her throat, sinking lower, edging the fragile fabric of her robe aside. The butterfly kisses he rained over the slope of her breast intensified the ache. Surely she'd be cured of the urge to be near him after this. She'd be rid of the desire to feel her fingers against his flesh.

"Let me touch," she whispered. "Please." Leaning forward in his arms, she grasped the first button of his shirt, slid it through the opening and pressed her mouth to the heat of his skin. Her fingers parted the fabric, crushed the soft hair on his chest.

"Rebecca," he groaned, pulling her back for another open-mouthed kiss. "I want you like I haven't wanted anything in years. You're killing me with those lips of yours, love."

He kissed her again, nipping, licking, devouring her lips. He was hot and demanding and absolutely commanding. She could feel herself starting to slip away and she cared not a whit. She who had fought so hard to maintain her identity.

But when he shifted and the slick material of her robe sent her sliding slightly on his lap, she felt the heat and hardness of him beneath her. She looked directly into his eyes and saw…golden fire. She witnessed need and want and pain, the very thing she was sure he saw mirrored in her.

For a second she hesitated.

The tug-of-war intensified. She ached to press close and experience the wonder of making love with Logan, even though it would be a big step, maybe an irreparable step. She wasn't sure who or what she would be after she had lain in Logan's arms. She was pretty sure that once the ecstasy had died down, she would be feeling a lot of things she really didn't want to feel.

And yet…she bit down on her lip, looked into his deep, darkening eyes, leaned closer, breathing in the essence of the man.

Her fingers hovered on the white edges of his lapel, her will torn. Then he gathered both her hands in one of his own. He let out a low groan and lifted her from him, shifting his body away. With what could only be the touch of experience, he quickly closed her kimono and put her back together.

"Logan?"

"My fault, sweetheart. I'd promised I wouldn't touch you again."

"I could have stopped it."

"Only with a very definitive 'no,' and we both know that you were still wrapped up in the aftereffects of your movie."

She opened her mouth to protest that she had known what she was doing, to take her share of the blame, but he leaned closer, the look in his eyes begging her not to say more.

"I'm not apologizing for kissing you, Rebecca. I've been wanting to taste you again and it was probably far better to get a small taste and leave it at that than to let the longing build until I completely lost control, but the fact is that we both know going farther would be a mistake. You're not a woman who wanders through dark woods meeting with wolves who take what they want and move on. I'm not a man who steals cookies and milk from innocents."

She blinked hard at that, tucked her chin in and crossed her arms. "I've been married, Logan. I'm hardly an innocent."

His smile was disarming, heartbreaking. He gently smoothed back her hair, which had fallen forward onto her cheek. "You're a highly intelligent, accomplished woman, Rebecca. I'm trusting you with one of my greatest treasures," he said, holding one hand out to emphasize the building. "But you'll have to trust me on this. Marriage doesn't have anything to do with the end of innocence. It's a state of mind, not a state of marriage, love. You'll be an innocent when you're beautifully old, still driving the wolves mad to have you."

"So you're a wolf?" she asked, managing a smile at the chagrin in his voice. In spite of the need still churning within her, she was sure she should be grateful that Logan had used more common sense than she had. For a moment there, she had forgotten just how dangerous her emotions could be.

"I'm a wolf who's trying very badly to behave," he agreed, rising to his feet. "So I think it's best if I leave now, Rebecca."

He turned to go.

"Logan?"

Looking back over his shoulder, he raised one brow.

"Thank you," she said quietly, "for making me take some breathing time today. And for kissing me and then stopping even though neither of us wanted to."

He groaned. "Rebecca," he warned, "you do not want to make comments like that to a wolf. Believe me."

She shook her head. "I trust you, Logan. And I think you're right about my taking some rest time now and then. If you and I avoided each other less, the urge to touch might be less strong. So I'll take some time from now on, and—"

He gazed into her eyes. Fiercely. Waiting for her to make her move, like the leader of the pack he was.

"And?"

"Tomorrow we'll take some downtime. Races in the pool after work."

She grinned wickedly.

Her wolf looked slightly...unsure.

"If we play, we can keep it light, keep it smart," she said.

"And we definitely want to keep things smart," he agreed. "You trust me?"

"Implicitly."

He took a deep and visible breath. "I'll do my best to maintain that trust then, Red."

"Red?"

"Innocent," he drawled. "Don't go walking in any more woods tonight, love."

He left her. She looked at the screen, looked at the remote. She had planned to watch another movie, but somehow the hero seemed to pall next to her real-life wolf.

She wondered what things he had seen and done in his life to convince himself that he was that bad, that dangerous.

"But he is dangerous, Linden," she whispered. "Not many women wouldn't follow him into the woods gladly even if it meant a broken heart, even if it meant forgetting all the smart lessons of a lifetime. A woman might turn herself into a pretzel trying to be what that man wanted. And when he moved on, she'd be a mess.''

Something to think about. Something to think about long and hard, she thought, flicking off the lights and trailing upstairs to her room.

Logan had given her the gift of an easy exit. She'd be a fool not to take it.

And Rebecca had never been a fool.

Chapter Seven

The countdown had begun. With the grand opening only five days away, Logan wasn't sure which countdown had taken the forefront in his mind, however: the opening of this hotel or the day he and Rebecca would part ways and he would start thinking like a sane, rational man again.

Because darn it, there was no real reason for him to be so edgy. This particular hotel might be his baby, the most important hotel he'd opened since his first, but he was still an old hand at these things. He had amassed enough money that one failure wouldn't be more than an irritating nick in his pride. He'd certainly had more than his share of experience with women, so there was absolutely no sane explanation for why he was feeling somewhat tense as he neared the pool.

"Only mind-melting, nonstop, take-no-prisoners unrequited lust," he muttered as he pulled back the door. That had to be all it was.

Then he looked up and saw Rebecca. She was sitting on the edge of the pool and waving at him. Nothing at all outrageous about her. The lady wore a simple black tank suit, not too low at the neck, not too high on the legs. That silky chestnut hair of hers wasn't hooked seductively behind her ear, no curls brushing low to draw attention to her breasts. No come-hither look in the lady's eyes. So how come he was this close to marching over there and scooping her up in his arms? And why was it that her brilliant smile made everything tighten inside his body until the pain in his chest was raw and wild?

Pure insanity, Brewster, he thought.

"You're late, Brewster," she said with a sassy grin, pointing to her watch and reaching up over her head to twist all that thick chestnut hair into a rope and clip it out of the way. "That means I get to call the weapons." She wrinkled her nose at him, daring him to argue with her.

He grinned back, holding up both hands in protest. "I'm on time, lady. You've just got that darn watch of yours set ahead so you're always on top of things three minutes before you have to be. Pete told me your sweet little secrets the last time I was in the gym. And what exactly do you mean by weapons?"

But she was already scurrying up from her perch by the time the words were completely out of his mouth. Her little fanny swayed as she walked toward a storage bench on the side and began to rummage through it.

"Diving sticks," she proclaimed in triumph, coming up with three bright fluorescent plastic rods. "And if you're very good, Logan, maybe even some kickboards later."

Her soft, low voice dipped into his consciousness and he wondered just how good he had to be and what he had to be good at. Suddenly something as mundane as a kickboard sounded like the promise of pure pleasure. He had the feeling Rebecca could make eating oatmeal sound like an erotic experience. And the darnedest thing was that she wasn't even trying.

But before he could examine that phenomenon any further, she had twisted off the cap of the sticks, filled them with water, recapped them and tossed them into the pool.

"You ready?" she said, lifting one brow in challenge.

He raised one corner of his lips. "Any particular rules?"

She shrugged. "No pushing or shoving and no fair not having fun. The one with the most rods wins."

And with a quick smile over her shoulder to make sure that he agreed, she counted down from five to one and both of them plunged into the pool.

The lady was like a lithe little fish, Logan thought, as she kicked off toward the end of the pool. He aimed for the other, snagged the green rod and headed for the blue one, which had fallen in at the nine-foot depth.

He was just reaching out for the blue rod when a flash of black and pink circled round him and then reached out.

Fingertips touched. For a second Rebecca let go of the rod, and Logan, aware that she had let go rather than risk physical contact with him again, let go as well. The rod began to sink, and the lady snatched it up and kicked upward toward the surface.

Her legs swished past him. He followed like a stallion on the scent of a mare and broke surface right behind her.

"I won," she said triumphantly with a wide smile.

"You did," he agreed.

"Oh, come on," she said, cheerfully splashing water his way. "Aren't you even going to dispute my call? You had it full in your grasp for half a second. Where's that killer instinct that made you a successful hotel baron? No one likes to win too easily."

She was smiling at him, all dimples and challenge. He remembered the day they'd played pool.

"I dropped it," he reminded her.

"I'm not sure you didn't do that on purpose. That gentleman that resides inside you. The diplomatic hotelier who makes sure that the customer always leaves satisfied."

He shook the water out of his hair, smiling all the while. "The kids I used to play poker with on the streets would be...interested to know how fair I've become in my game playing. A gentlemen, you say? A diplomat?"

"You let me win, Logan."

He hadn't, not really. He'd been just as affected by that zap of sensation that had coursed through him at her touch as she had. But he could see that the lady wanted her satisfaction, and he intended for her to have it. He was, above all, a man who knew how to compete, how to fight to win, and if that was what the lady wanted and needed to wipe that unsettling touch out of her memory, he wanted her to have it.

He raised his chin in a gesture of daring. "Okay, Rebecca. You're on. Rematch." And he tossed the green rod he was still holding in a great graceful arc that sent it directly to the bottom of the deep end.

Her instant chuckle was his reward. And for the next hour or two, they dived, they surfaced, they dragged out the kickboards that eliminated his advantage of greater upper-body strength and had neck-or-nothing races from one end of the pool to the other.

He lost some, won some and gloated shamelessly over his successes.

"You didn't have to crow about that last one," she protested, as they floated side by side, their upper bodies resting on the buoyant bits of plastic foam. "I was only an eighth of an inch behind you."

"It was as tough a competition as I've ever been in," he admitted, but suddenly her smile faded away.

"I suppose you've been in some fairly tough competitions. Was your life—what was your life like when you were a child?" she asked, her voice just a breath louder than the lapping of the water as they languidly kicked now and then to keep themselves afloat.

Okay, careful here now, Brewster. You've seen how the lady is affected by less than lucky kids. And you know she's got plenty of stress in her life right now. No need for her to have to shadow box hurts that have already faded into the distant past.

He lifted one shoulder in a casual shrug and made for the side of the pool. "It was a childhood, Rebecca. No different from those lots of other kids have."

But she had followed him. Like him, she was pulling herself out of the water, sitting on the side. "You said you grew up on the streets. I don't know many kids who do that."

"Lots of them do. Makes you strong."

"Before you should have to be strong."

"Rebecca..." he drawled.

"Your parents…"

Okay, she wanted details. He'd give her the short version.

"No father. Have no clue who he was, just that my mother loved him and he didn't feel the same. I had a mother. Things turned out fine." End of story.

He thought that pretty much said it all. It should be enough, but she had that soft, worried look in those big violet eyes of hers. "Just that? Just I had a mother? Is she…gone?"

"Years ago. She died soon after I opened my second hotel."

She nodded slightly. "She must have been proud of you."

The woman had hated his guts. But Rebecca wanted and needed to think that he'd had a caring parent, and he wanted Rebecca to be happy, so he found a smile somewhere.

"How about you, sweet stuff? You mentioned your less-than-pleasant aunt and uncle, but you also told me you'd been loved and married. Tell me something about your loving husband."

That would bring back her smile, he hoped. Warm happy memories of a man who'd thought she made the world turn on its axis. It made *him* happy to know that someone had been there to wipe away the memory of the adults who should have taken better care of her.

She shook her head. "James was a wonderful man. He married me knowing I didn't love him as deeply as he loved me. I think he hoped that my feelings would grow into that kind of love. Instead I was grateful to him and I admired him," she said, staring into Logan's eyes as if she needed him to know she hadn't been cold to the man who'd pledged his heart and future to her. "I think—no, I know I hurt him."

"You couldn't hurt a gnat."

"Maybe not on purpose, but...by accident? Yes. James knew about my aunt and uncle. He thought of me as a princess he was rescuing from a tower. He was a gentle man, ten years older than me, and he'd been waiting for one woman, for a princess all his life. He didn't expect a woman who loved to play pool and win at races and sing loudly and pound on the piano, and he didn't criticize me, really, but in his heart, he desperately loved the fantasy woman he wanted me to be. He was a very sad man. I think he kept hoping I'd change and that I'd learn to love him the way he needed to be loved."

Logan felt a slow, simmering anger building within him.

"Don't go thinking that was your fault, Rebecca. You can't be responsible for other people's dreams."

She looked directly at him. "Maybe not, but maybe if I'd been paying more attention, I would have seen that there was a problem before I married him. Maybe I wouldn't have married him then, but...maybe I would have, anyway. I needed saving pretty badly at that time."

She took a deep breath and pasted on a too-wide smile. "Anyway, that was years ago. I'm very independent now. No need to be saved. No sense in reliving past mistakes. I'm content with my life, very happy, but I don't ever want to be like James," she said slowly. "I don't want that kind of all-consuming love."

There was a sadness in her voice, even though she was smiling, and Logan realized that even though she didn't deserve it, this lady lived with a great deal of guilt. And he wanted to chase that sadness away.

"Hey, Red," he said gently, brushing one finger across her cheek. "While we've been playing and talking, the clock's hands have been spinning in a circle. More than once. Guess we're going to have to hustle now. Last one to the other side has to explain to Jarvis why we're late for dinner," he said, motioning toward the clock.

She blinked and looked at the clock. "Yikes, who would have thought it was that late?" The sadness fled in the rush of the moment. She looked at him suspiciously, but then she pushed off the side of the pool, catching him off guard and skimming ahead.

"I win," she said when she reached the side.

But he looked at her smile and thought, No, lady, I definitely win this time. He nodded in acquiescence.

She frowned. "Come on," she whispered conspiratorially. "You're doing it again. Letting me cheat. You know darn well I didn't play fair. We'll go throw ourselves on Jarvis's mercy together, and hope that he doesn't serve us sawdust to punish us."

"And ruin his reputation?"

She nodded in agreement. "You're right. Wouldn't happen. So, what do you think? Triple-chocolate-fudge cake for dessert?"

"With cherries," he agreed. "It'll be torture, but with a little luck, we'll survive."

Her soft laughter chased all the clouds away and Logan was able to look across the candles at dinner that night and realize just what a survivor, what a treasure he'd had the pleasure to find at that auction.

Except for the fact that he knew the lady's full worth when her dreamer husband obviously hadn't, he did know a small measure of what James might have felt. Because loving this lady would no doubt be like trying to love a sunbeam. Wonderful and yet impossible. She didn't want to ever face the dangers of love. And of course, neither did he, Logan reminded himself. He definitely didn't want to fall in love with Rebecca Linden.

Rebecca wondered if all grand-opening days were this tense, if Logan felt as she did, that his heart had climbed so high in his throat that simple breathing was all but impossible.

Since that day at the pool, they'd worked more closely, more as a team and yet with a distance. She knew now how completely lethal getting close to this man could be. This was a man who'd coaxed her into spilling her secrets when she never offered up those tidbits from her past. And without even trying, without even pressuring her in any way. He'd simply asked and she had responded. It was a frightening thought, to speculate what she'd give up if only this man asked.

What's more, he hadn't fooled her with that non-answer to her question about his mother being proud of him. Logan Brewster had lived a hard life with an uncaring mother, Rebecca would bet. In her line of work, she met too many young tough guys who were only tough because it kept them from breaking inside. That was Logan as a kid, she'd bet her secretary's chair. And now she was thinking about him all the time, worrying about him, wanting to be near him. She felt for the little boy he must have been, felt deep pride for the man he'd become. She realized those feelings held a dagger-sharp danger for her. He'd been tantalizing before when she had simply known he was a kind, caring, wildly attractive man. Now he was more. Suddenly what had been a job she wanted to do well had become a mission. She wanted to make this special for Logan. His tenth hotel, a hotel that would naturally hold a certain amount of sentiment for him. In a case like that, little things could make all the difference.

And so she'd been up since first sun getting ready. She'd had a short meeting with Emily and Caroline, a minor crisis when a fashion-blind Emily had needed help choosing a special outfit for an outing with Simon, but that hadn't taken very long, and since then all Rebecca's efforts had been centered on the hotel. As the doors to the Oaks opened to the public for the very first time, she was at Logan's side, determined to do everything she could to make this his best grand opening ever.

"Are you ready?" she whispered.

He looked down at her, those drowning gold eyes staring into hers. "Shh, love," he said, taking her hand. "You look beautiful. You *are* beautiful inside and out and it always shows. Everything will be fine."

His steady gaze, his touch calmed her, made her remember that she wanted to help *him*. He should not have to worry about her.

She stood taller, stepped forward to greet an elderly woman encrusted in pearls and flowered silk whose bags were being carried in. "You must be Mrs. Winslow. Welcome to the Oaks. I'm Rebecca Linden and I'm here to make sure your stay is all that you want it to be. We're so glad to have you here."

"It's a lovely hotel, isn't it?" the woman said. She

smiled at Rebecca and gestured to all the sparkling glass that let in the sunlight and turned the flowers and fountains and blue sky like interior into a summer day coaxed inside and come to life.

Rebecca smiled her agreement. "I'm probably biased, but it's the most lovely hotel I've ever been in, and I'm sure you'll find that it's the most comfortable, too. We're here to make your stay as pleasant as possible, so just ask if you need anything. I understand you like to knit or read to relax, so you'll find a supply of various yarns and knitting supplies in your room, a selection of novels and, of course, your favorite lemon tea, but if there's anything else you need, I'll do my best to lend a hand."

The woman looked up at Logan and grinned. "You didn't give me lemon tea last time, Logan."

He chuckled. "You never mentioned you like it, Cecily, or you know it would have been yours at the snap of a finger. But I guess it took Rebecca to ferret out that little tidbit. I'm sure you'll find she'll be the jewel that makes this stay with us special."

Cecily Winslow grinned at Rebecca. "Isn't he a doll?"

Rebecca felt the heat climbing up her throat, but she managed to smile. "I have the feeling some of the ladies would rather have him than lemon tea."

The woman's slightly raspy laughter rang out. "You're right, Logan. She's a jewel."

Then Mrs. Winslow allowed herself to be led away to her room.

Rebecca felt herself relaxing. "She was very nice, wasn't she?"

Logan placed one hand on the small of her back and applied a slight reassuring touch. "They're just

people, Rebecca. And now that they're more than
names in the database, you can see that. They're all
just people, most of them very nice."

It was true. Rebecca ignored Tony Revere's designer sunglasses that had probably cost more than
her car and asked him about his golf game. She assured him that she had scouted out all the local
courses and left a list with ratings in his room. She
asked Agnes Farrell about her grandchildren and sat
with her then and there to ooh and aah over the pic-
tures of the gorgeous little darlings who were on vacation with their parents in St. Kitts. She found herself
agreeing to watch an old movie with Melanie Stivers
so the lady wouldn't have to watch it alone.

And through all of this, Logan circled, chatting
with his guests, renewing old acquaintances, striking
up conversations with new ones. Easily. Charmingly.

She noticed that he was frequently at her elbow,
introducing her, making things easier for her, even
though there were few difficult guests. And even then,
she managed.

The only time she saw Logan lose his smile at all
was when a young wealthy family of four entered the
lobby. The husband was belting out orders to his wife,
who was obviously stressed. When the woman started
screeching loudly at her son, who looked to be about
nine and was fidgeting, Rebecca felt Logan stiffen at
her side. She looked up and saw that his face had
gone tight. He started to step forward, then stopped
as if his feet had rooted themselves to the marble
floor.

Rebecca glided forward, smiled at the child and
held out her hand to the woman who was looking a
bit flustered at being stopped in midsentence. "Hello.

Welcome. I'm Rebecca Linden. We just want to let all the parents know that we're providing a special service for families. Knowing how hectic things get at arrival, we've set up an area with all sorts of things designed for the children's amusement. It's well supervised by two former teachers and we provide pagers for our parents. Would you—that is, perhaps your son would like to explore there a bit while you get settled in and have a chance to relax. If that would be all right with you, of course.''

A guilty look crept into both the man's and woman's eyes. ''I'm afraid we've been on the road a bit long,'' the woman said. ''And yes, we all do need a chance to soothe our nerves. Thank you. Would you like to have some time to play, Evan?''

He nodded quickly. ''Sure, mom. Sorry about pinching Nina,'' he said, looking to his little sister.

Rebecca smiled at the family. ''I always need a long nap and time to put my feet up after I've been on the road awhile,'' she said. ''Let's see what we can do to make you more comfortable.'' She gave the parents the location where they could find the game room and made her way back to Logan's side.

''Logan, I—that is, they're all right,'' she said, studying his expression.

''Of course. And thank you. Dealing with tense family situations isn't exactly my strength.''

Which only made Rebecca wonder more about what kinds of things he'd gone through, because she had seen him handling much more difficult situations this day. A woman with five yapping dogs. A man whose suitcase exploded just inside the door. A family who insisted on having their room moved four times.

He continued to handle his guests with ease and patience throughout the rest of the afternoon. Finally, there was a lull in the rush and he made his way back over to her.

"Sorry to have left you to the charms of Bill Errins," Logan apologized when things had more or less cleared out. "He's a bit grouchy at times."

She shrugged. "It was okay. I just shrunk him to the size of a whiny eight-year-old in my mind, and after that it was easy. He just needed someone to be a bit firm with him."

A smile flitted over Logan's lips. "And what exactly did you tell him?"

She twisted at the button on the top of her blue dress. "Nothing much. Only that I was sure that he must be tired and that I was positive he'd feel much better after a nice bath and a long nap. And then I had him whisked away to his room. Kind of an adult time-out, you know."

He grinned, and she twisted the button harder.

"Do you think that was too obvious?"

"I think it was perfect. Don't do that, love," he whispered, leaning forward and stilling her hands with his own. "Don't—just don't twist that button any farther. It's liable to fall off, and then there'll be hell to pay. It wouldn't do for the owner of the Oaks to peel back the lapels on his assistant's dress and kiss his way down her body right here in the middle of the lobby."

Rebecca immediately removed her fingers from the button. She looked up into storm-dark eyes. For a moment she wanted to sway forward right here where everyone could see. She wanted him to kiss her, to touch her. But he was right. They were on display—

and they'd both decided that it was not smart for them to touch too much at all, in the lobby or anywhere else.

"I'll be careful, Logan," she promised.

He stepped away and put on his Eldora Oaks smile. "You were perfect today, Rebecca. Thank you. Everything was perfect."

But as she moved away to take care of a few details that had been called to her attention, she realized that everything was *not* perfect. She was helping Logan, and that was good. He was experiencing success, and that was good. But more and more, she was wanting him to touch her, to smile at her, to share the deepest parts of himself with her. She was beginning to feel like her world orbited around Logan Brewster, and that just wouldn't do. She was nothing like the women he usually sought out for his pleasure, and she'd promised she would never try to make herself over again. More importantly, she didn't want to be like James, wanting the unattainable, loving where love couldn't be returned. And that was exactly what would happen if she let herself fall for Logan. He might want her for a while, he might enjoy her company, even admire her as she had admired her husband, but Logan Brewster had made it clear he didn't want love or family. Every time he saw a child, he tensed. He clearly would never choose to have any of his own. She'd be a total fool to let herself fall any further.

It was definitely time to call Deb at Summerstaff again and see if any new jobs had come up. Work would take her mind off the man and off her problems, just as it always had. For sure.

Chapter Eight

"Okay, sweetheart, we're taking you out of here."
The deep, distinct chords of Logan's voice swept over
Rebecca several days later, and for a second she simply savored the sound of him. She loved the shivers
that passed through her whenever he spoke, even
though she knew she would pay for that particular
weakness. She'd crave his voice someday when it was
no longer available.

But the man was simply talking nonsense.

"I can't go anywhere, Logan. There's too much to
do here." She held out a pad of paper with her list
of "Things That Should Have Been Done Yesterday."

He took it from her fingers and tossed it to the
nearest bellhop. "Don't lose this, Joe, okay? The lady
might get violent if I deprive her of her work."

"I'll guard it like it's golden," Joe promised.

Logan smiled his thanks. "And now," he said,
turning to Rebecca. "Let's talk about the fact that

you're supposed to take time off now and then. Didn't we discuss this once before?''

"That was before the guests arrived."

"Yes, and they're going to be very grouchy guests if they think we're tracking their every move. Relax, love. You know as well as I do that we have daytime and evening staff. The morning shift has just come on, fresh and ready to help any guests who need help. The activities are all scheduled for the evening so that people can go sight-seeing during the daytime. You've provided all the information anyone will need to see the delights of the area, and there are plenty of Oaks employees who are waiting to answer questions. For now, you need to rest."

She opened her mouth to protest.

Okay, he knew her by now. Logan grinned. "If you don't rest, you won't be fresh tonight when you need to be. All those performers to be orchestrated this evening, remember?"

She looked just the slightest bit uncertain. Time to go in for the kill.

"And I've heard that there's an art fair in town today and your friends Emily and Caroline will be there."

Uh oh. Suspicion. "How do you know that?"

He raised one brow. "I have my spies."

She raised her brow right back at him. "No doubt spying is a skill you learned on the streets as a boy."

"Absolutely," he agreed. "And a very handy skill, too."

She stopped looking anxiously at Joe who still had her to-do pad. "Did you have any bright moments as a child, Logan?"

Not many. He searched his brain for some lighter

moments, gently took her arm and started to lead her toward the door. It was fortunate that the lady was wearing white slacks. For what he had in mind a dress just wouldn't do and if he gave her time to go back to her room, she'd find a million details that she'd insist needed tending.

"I had a friend named Deets who could juggle anything. We picked up some fine money on the street that way. And he even taught me a little."

"You can juggle?"

He shrugged. "Not much, but some." She was staring up at him. He led her out the side door to the pavilion.

"Will you show me?" Those wide violet eyes were open wider with interest now, making him crazy, leading him down seductive paths when he needed to keep his mind on getting Rebecca out into some restful sunshine.

"I'll show you," he promised. "Sometime. But for now, the art fair." He looked at Andy who ran the pavilion, held up two fingers, gave a quick nod to Rebecca, and the smiling young man gave him the thumbs-up sign.

Immediately a small frown formed on Rebecca's lips. "What are we—" She looked around her as if she hadn't even noticed her surroundings until now. "You're very slick, Mr. Brewster. Have I told you that? You know very well I was paying so much attention to what you were saying that I didn't even notice where we were going. You would have made a fine pickpocket, I'll bet." Her slightly disgruntled tone let him know that now was probably not the best time to tell her that he'd once been quite an accomplished pickpocket. "You were trying to distract me.

I'll bet you can't even juggle,'' she said with a smile as she let Andy adjust the bicycle he had brought around.

"Wait. I'll prove it to you someday, sweetheart," Logan whispered near her ear as he climbed on the bicycle and led the way out of the hotel complex.

"Don't make empty promises, Logan. I've had plenty of kids try that, and I make it a point of holding them to their word. Builds character. And gets me what I want, too."

He looked at her and saw that she was smiling fully now, clearly enjoying herself.

"I have it on good word that you like riding bikes."

"I get around town like that a lot of times," she agreed. "Keeps me in shape and besides, I like the wind in my hair."

As if she had Mother Nature's ear, the breeze lifted her locks at just that moment, blowing a wisp of hair back over her shoulder. Tempting a man to touch if he hadn't been on a two-wheeled instrument of torture, Logan thought, pedaling along beside her. No way was he ever going to tell her that he'd rarely ridden a bike in his life. No money for one when he was a kid. No sense in wasting a good Jaguar once he became an adult. But if the lady liked to pedal, they'd pedal.

Down the long, looping road that led into town, they rode side by side where they could, single file when a car came along.

"So you've heard that Emily and Caroline will be here today. How do you know that?"

He grinned. "Simple. Emily's spending her time working for Simon Cantrell whose family employs a

good part of the town, and Caroline is working for
Gideon Tremayne who has a prosperous business of
his own and the added mystique of being the grandson of a knight. People pay attention to the plans of
the rich and famous. Word gets around and I happen
to employ a number of the townspeople who like to
talk about what's going on in the heart of the town."

She tilted her head in agreement. "I suppose that
makes sense. Do those people ever mention my
friends? I mean, do they know how Emily and Caroline are faring?"

"You don't?"

"I know what they tell me, but we're a bit like
sisters. They're not going to tell me anything that
might worry me too much."

"And you think you might have reason to worry?"

She tightened her hands on the handlebars. "I don't
know. As you say, the men they're working for are
fairly rich and powerful. I hear they're both quite
charming."

She looked at him as if to see if he agreed. He was
frowning slightly. "You haven't met them?"

"Only momentarily. Anyway, I'm just a bit...
concerned. Em and Caroline and I have always traveled the road together, but we all have pretty serious
goals of our own. Emily is determined to open a
school for young single mothers, Caroline is an accomplished writer when she's not teaching and she
wants to marry and have a huge noisy family. Neither
of those activities would seem to fit in with getting
involved with a rich, confirmed bachelor."

"Caroline's a bit like you then?"

She swung wide to avoid a puddle. "A bit, but
Caroline is more intent on making a partnership of a

marriage. No love desired or required. More of a business relationship devoted to the business of raising babies. I'm probably the most conventional of all of us. I do want marriage based on love, just not the usual kind people associate with a marriage. And I'd settle for just a few children. But what about *your* friends? Whatever happened to your friend Deets?"

The only sound for a few seconds was the whirring of the wheels.

"Logan?"

He looked up into her eyes and smiled to let her know he was all right. "I'm afraid he died. But it was a long time ago, Rebecca. I was just a kid."

"How old?"

He choked the handlebars, his knuckles turning white. "Twelve." Because he could see the question in her eyes and knew the worry would gnaw at her if he said nothing, he pedaled his bike closer. "His father beat him regularly. It wasn't that unusual in the neighborhood where I came from, but I usually wasn't there when it happened. Deets was, well, we were the same age, but he was physically a lot smaller than I was, and his father was a big guy. We came in late one day, and the man started hitting him. Over and over. I jumped on his father, and I hit him as hard as I could. It wasn't much but it was enough for Deets to get away. The next day, Deets fell down a flight of stairs, they said. He died before I could say goodbye."

"Did you—did you tell the police about the incident with the father?"

He stared at her, wishing he could end the story the way she wanted it to end. "Both Deets and I had been in trouble for one thing or another too many times. The police knew us. It was only the word of a sometime juvenile thief against that of an adult. I've always wondered what would have happened if I'd simply let Deets's stepdad beat him up that first day, if I hadn't humiliated the man in front of his kid.''

She stopped her bicycle dead in the street, reaching out her hand as he stopped too. ''You did the right thing, Logan.''

He shook his head. ''The crazy thing was that it wasn't the first time I stepped in like that and someone else got a worse beating because of it. I was an angry and stubborn kid, Rebecca, and sometimes not a very wise one.''

''No one's wise when they're twelve, Logan.''

But they were where he came from. Kids learned wisdom early. It was a matter of survival, and he'd—finally—learned how to be wise. Don't get too involved with anyone. Don't let anyone under your skin that you wouldn't mind losing down the road. Don't keep any doors open too wide. He'd almost forgotten that rule lately. He'd have to try harder to remember.

''*You're* a very wise lady, Rebecca,'' he said, dredging up a smile to please her.

''That I am, Logan, and don't you forget it,'' she said with a tentative smile of her own.

They started off again, sailed down into the grassy area where the art fair was taking place. They parked their bikes and strolled amid displays of the works of painters and craftsmen. Rebecca admired a sketch of a boy who looked a lot like her young friend, Jack, and Logan made a point of remembering who and where the artist was.

When she finally came upon Emily and Caroline, the three of them gathered together and hugged and exchanged questions about one another's situation. It seemed that Emily and her Simon were throwing a party for Simon's aunt's birthday in just a few days, and Caroline was helping Gideon entertain a houseful of guests, including Gideon's sister. All of the women were lovely. All of them looked slightly tense.

While they talked he turned around to look at a display of ornamental birdhouses. He was just wondering how they'd look in the trees at the Oaks when he felt a presence at his elbow.

"Excuse me for asking. Em and I appreciate your contributions to Summerstaff, but Rebecca is our roommate and, well, we've got to ask. You're not working her too hard, are you, Mr. Brewster?" He looked down to see a blue-eyed, auburn-haired beauty.

"Caroline O'Donald. I saw you from the distance when you picked up Rebecca at the apartment," she explained.

Then that would be Emily beside her, pulling Rebecca along. The women had apparently decided to move their conversation his way.

He grinned at Rebecca's friends. "Nice to meet you, ladies. And yes, I'm doing my best to convince Rebecca she doesn't owe me her life just because I made a donation to your cause," he agreed.

"And she's got plenty of personal space? Rebecca needs her space," the dark-haired Emily asked.

"Would you two stop it?" Rebecca asked, rolling her eyes. "I'm an adult. Tell them I'm an adult, Logan."

He grinned down at the two women. "Rebecca is an adult, even though she likes to cheat at races in the pool and loves to ride a bicycle instead of taxiing into town in one of the perfectly fine luxury cars I've left at her disposal.''

The other women were ignoring Rebecca's embarrassed protests.

"Relax, love, they're your friends. You know, you worry about them just as much as they do you. They're just making sure you're all right.''

"And about that personal space, Mr. Brewster?'' Emily repeated her request.

"The man has given me a suite, Em. I think I might have mentioned that, but thanks for asking anyway, sweetie. I know you're just looking out for me.''

Emily and Caroline looked from Rebecca to Logan and then back again. They didn't look completely happy as they held out their hands to shake Logan's.

"Just keep taking care of her, Logan. You're a big guy, but I figure if Em and I each tried our hardest, we could do a certain amount of damage,'' Caroline said.

He chuckled and shook both of their hands. "I'm glad Rebecca has such good friends. I'll worry about her less once I'm gone if I know someone is watching out for the wolves.''

The two women exchanged glances.

"Logan has this silly theory that I'm a bit too innocent for my own good,'' Rebecca explained weakly.

"Hey, I like it,'' Emily said.

"He's obviously a highly intelligent individual,'' Caroline agreed. "Nice to have met you, Logan. Sorry if we were rude. As it is, we'd stay to talk, but I'm here with Gideon and his sister and Emily is leaving in a few minutes, too. She and Simon have plans this afternoon.''

Caroline went on her way with a wave. Emily stayed to talk a few minutes longer. Gideon Tremayne made a short appearance, but soon enough Rebecca and Logan were once again alone.

Rebecca looked at him long and hard.

"Well, that was a bit embarrassing, wasn't it?"

He chuckled. "As I said, they're your friends, Rebecca. I'm glad you have good ones."

It was true. Having met her caring friends, he would worry a little less about her future. But, Logan figured, it was a given that he was still going to worry some no matter what. At least until the lady's memory faded.

The Grand Opening was going just fine. Rebecca had gotten her picture from Jack in the mail yesterday. A sweet, big-eyed portrait of his little sister. There'd been a short note as well, and he'd seemed reasonably happy. She knew she should have been pleased, and she was, but she also couldn't stop thinking about what Logan had revealed to her when they biked into town this morning.

He'd lost his best friend when he was only twelve. And no matter what he'd said, she knew that he felt responsible. What would that kind of guilt and loss and grief do to a lonely, street-tough boy? Especially to a boy who'd already been deprived of the kind of parental love that every child should have?

Walls, she thought. He'd built walls around his heart. Immovable walls, high ones, thick ones. Walls that couldn't ever be torn down. He wouldn't risk getting involved, he wouldn't ever want to be responsible for a child's welfare again. He wouldn't want love, because love left you vulnerable. Love could open an old wound that might never be closed afterward.

"Oh, Logan," she whispered as she got ready for the evening. The man was all charm, all smiles. He had to be to be as successful at his business as he was, but it was all on the surface. Nothing could get to the heart of him. He wouldn't let it. She really needed to remember that for her own sake. Yet she was determined to—somehow—show him that his goodness went a little deeper than he suspected. He'd been kind to her, he was good to his employees, and whether he realized it or not, he was still stepping in to help kids. She had an idea of how to demonstrate that much to him, and so she picked up the phone and made a quick call.

"Life can't be all work, Logan," she said, smiling to herself. "If you can drag me out of the hotel to help me relax, I can drag you somewhere for your own good, too."

Tomorrow she'd show him, but tonight she had a dozen performances to oversee.

Logan weighed the diamond-and-sapphire necklace in his hand and thought about what it would look like on Rebecca. That tawny hair spread over a pillow, those big expressive violet eyes, and the sparkling jewels around her neck, dipping low between her bare breasts. Swaying in an attempt to draw his attention from the beauty of her body—and failing miserably as he tumbled her onto her bed and kissed his way from her eyelids to the slender arch of her foot.

"That's enough, Brewster," he told himself, squeezing the jewels in his hand as he moved toward her room. The lady had scheduled an evening demanding enough without having to ward off his way-ward desires.

When she opened her door, she was smiling brilliantly, but he could detect a small trace of tension behind her eyes.

"Almost ready, Logan," she promised, sitting to slip on a pair of black heels with ankle straps. She bent to fasten the straps, and his attention was drawn to her legs, her delicate ankles, the way her fingers brushed her skin as she struggled with the slender clasp.

"Darn fake fingernails," she said, smiling up at him in embarrassment. "Be right there."

"Let me help, Rebecca," he said and without waiting for her reply, he dropped to one knee before her, gently removed her hand from the clasp and slid his own fingers there. Immediately he knew this had been a bad move, and way too impulsive. Her skin was soft, the sweet honeysuckle scent of her drifted around him and his eyes were at a level with the rise and fall of her breasts.

He heard the soft catch of her breath, worked to control his own breathing and quickly secured the straps.

She started to rise, but he stayed her with one touch of his hand.

"Not yet. Wait." He pulled the delicate necklace from the depths of his pocket.

She stared at it for a few seconds as if she didn't know quite what it was. Her eyelids fluttered nervously. But she shook her head slightly as if to clear it. Then she reached behind her neck hesitantly and attempted to remove the simple silver chain she was wearing. Her fingers trembled.

He looked down at the black silk sheath she was wearing. The diamonds and sapphires would look perfect with the dress and with the lady, but he knew what she was thinking. Rebecca had convinced herself that she was macaroni and cheese and hot dogs. The necklace would look right, but she'd feel uncomfortable, as if he was trying to dress her up like a doll.

He shook his head and started to put the necklace back in his pocket. "You look lovely as you are," he said quietly, and it was the truth. Even without any ornamentation at all, she would make every other woman in the room look drab.

She placed her hand over his own, turned it over, brushing his fingers until his hand opened.

"I didn't mean to be so sensitive," she said. "It's silly. The past is...the past."

She looked at him pointedly. He had a sudden feeling that they'd gone from talking about her to talking about him.

No way was he going in that direction again. He reached behind her and undid the clasp of her necklace, his fingers brushing against her skin. He did his best to ignore his own reaction and the way her lids drifted low as he worked. Quickly he fastened the diamonds at her throat, placed her silver chain on the dresser and held out his arm.

"The night's just beginning, Rebecca. It's a night for pleasure. Nothing too deep, nothing too serious."

"A night for music," she agreed, letting him lead her away.

It was a night that had gone perfectly, he thought much later, as he strolled past the harpist and the intrigued group of listeners watching her pluck the last heavenly notes from the gold instrument. He searched for Rebecca in the crowd as he had done many times that evening, and found her smiling, talking, saying her goodnights to the slowly departing guests, and seemingly at ease in the midst of this group of mostly born-to-wealth visitors.

Then as the guests drifted away he noticed Glenna Delmont trundling toward Rebecca, a look of purpose in the aging woman's overly made-up eyes.

"Ms. Linden?" the woman said, drawing Rebecca's genial attention her way.

"Yes, Ms. Delmont, may I help you in some way?"

"As a matter of fact, you may. I've been wondering all night, where on earth did you get that exquisite piece of jewelry?"

The suspicion in the woman's tone was evident. Rebecca's fingers automatically slid to her throat. Soft pink suffused her neck, rose to kiss her cheeks.

"Mr. Brewster is lending it to me," she said softly.

"Oh, I see," the woman said, and it was obvious that she didn't see anything good. "How...very nice of him. I did wonder. Not many people in your position would be able to afford such an article. It must be worth thousands."

"Ah, but then appearances can be deceiving, can't they, Glenna?" Logan said, coming up behind Rebecca close enough to almost touch her, far enough away to make a mockery of this somewhat vicious woman's suggestion.

The older lady laughed a bit condescendingly. "People like to say that, but what one sees, Mr. Brewster, is usually relatively close to the truth."

He tilted his head. "Maybe so, Glenna, but then there was the case of your grandmother, wasn't there?

Quite a lady, I've heard. To the casual observer, she might have appeared to be, well, I suppose the term back then would have been a kept woman, a performer on the stage, too. But in truth, she was a bit more than that. Who would have thought that a woman who danced in front of crowds wearing only a few feathers would have also been a member of one of Wicket County's oldest and most distinguished families? Those appearances, they can fool you, can't they?"

"I—my grandmother was—you don't know—I—" The woman's mouth was open as she glared at Logan and Rebecca.

Her husband choked, then laughed out loud. "Got you there, Glenna. Your grandmother really did leave a trail of gossip in her wake. And, Ms. Linden," the man said with a nod of his head, "I don't care where you got those baubles. You're a delight. Kind, courteous and a genuine help to every guest here. And I defy anyone to say a bad word about you. I believe my wife here owes you an apology and I'm sure she'll realize that after she's had a bit of time to think. Mr. Brewster," he said, as he led his speechless wife away, lecturing her quietly as they walked.

Rebecca shivered slightly. She looked up at Logan, her eyes wide and strained. "Thank you."

He shook his head. "Frank Delmont was right, you know. You're the best thing any of my hotels have ever seen. The woman had no right to make those comments."

"I'm wearing your jewels," she said simply. "Anyone might have thought the wrong thing."

"Then it's my fault, isn't it?"

She shook her head this time. "No, you were just setting a stage. I realized that."

"And so should everyone else."

She raised her chin. "You're right, of course. No one's fault."

"Except Glenna's. Don't forgive her too easily if she apologizes."

Rebecca shrugged. "I'm a pushover, Logan. And anyway, we'll see. She hasn't apologized yet."

Tilting his head in agreement, Logan leaned against the piano as the last guest waved goodnight. "The evening worked out wonderfully otherwise, though, Rebecca. You should be proud. You pulled all of this together."

"The music *was* lovely, wasn't it?" she asked, a bit of the starlight beginning to return to those eyes that had been distressed only a minute before.

"It was a treat," he agreed. "You get a chance to play on this yet?" He indicated the piano he was leaning against.

"Once or twice. I don't like to play now that the guests are here."

"Most of them have already toddled off to bed," he said, nodding to the empty room.

Rebecca looked up at the challenge in his eyes. She knew that he was trying to take her mind off the incident earlier. Frankly, he was succeeding. Just being in the same room with Logan took her mind off everything else.

But she didn't feel comfortable playing on this piano. She loved music, but she wasn't a concert pianist. Her aunt had berated her often enough for her lack of talent, for the way she practically welded her fingers to the keys, trying to lose herself in the music rather than aiming for perfection.

"I'd like to hear you play, Rebecca. Just once. I won't expect miracles. Not at all. But I know you have music in your soul. I've heard you singing and humming too many times not to know that. Tonight I'd like to hear that again."

That was all it took. His comment recalled to her something her mother had told her many years ago, that it was the music in a person's soul that really counted.

She sat at the piano and she played for Logan. She tried to make the music for him that he must have missed out on as a child, the music of the soul that every child should hear, should live by and be given the gift of, every single day. She lost herself in the music—for this man. It wouldn't be enough to change the past. Nothing she could ever do could wipe out that sadness, break down those walls. But she needed to try to give him back a small bit of the gift he'd given her a few moments ago when he had leaped to her defense with golden fire in his eyes and the chill of winter in his deep voice.

And so she played.

Logan watched her, listened. She caressed the keys as a woman would caress her lover, Logan thought, watching Rebecca as she closed her eyes and softly stroked and pressed and slid her hands over the keyboard of the stately instrument. The soft, yearning strains of "Someone to Watch Over Me" flowed out into the room, filling his thoughts and his soul.

The music swirled around him as he watched her lithe form and he saw the joy of the experience transform her beautiful features into breathtaking rapture.

He watched and listened and practiced slow, deep breathing.

When the lady finally lifted her fingers from the keys, the last notes fading into the sudden stillness, he bent, he brushed her lips with his own, he indulged himself for one swift second, savoring all the beauty of the lady, inside and out. The wolf stole the touch he just had to have. And then, as she opened her eyes and reached up to touch the lips he'd just kissed, he grinned.

"Play something fast, Red," he said, reaching out to the basket of perfect fruit lying on the nearest table. As he balanced an apple, an orange and a pear in one hand, her smile finally came through.

"Show me, Logan," she said with delight as she struck up a fast show tune and he prayed he would remember how to keep three objects spinning through the air without dropping them. When he bid Rebecca good-night, he wanted her to remember this evening as a success, as a brief but enjoyable few hours.

Not the cruel comments of one thoughtless woman and not that quick lapse of his lips covering hers. Because the days were passing swiftly. Rebecca's time here was almost done and so was his. When she left, he wanted there to be no regrets on either side. When they looked back, he wanted them both to be able to remember just the smiles, the laughter and the fleeting moments of joy as they moved on into the rest of their lives apart.

Just focus on the pleasure of the moment, he thought as he kept his eyes on the whirling objects. *Don't look back. Don't look forward.* It was a philosophy that had always worked for him in the past. No reason why it shouldn't work just fine now.

Chapter Nine

"Are you still of the philosophy that a person should get out and play during the day?" Rebecca said, marching up to Logan after she'd lain in wait for him for a good hour. Honestly, the man lectured her about not working too hard, but he very rarely stopped moving himself. He had just finished putting Dave Elstrom, his physically recovering and somewhat functional manager, through the paces on local traditions and sights, and earlier he'd been down to check on a problem with the pool filter. He'd given concert tickets to a man who had been complaining that he'd thought there would be more activities planned for the guests, and consulted with Jarvis on a new recipe the man was thinking of trying out.

He pulled up in front of her, flashing her a grin. "Your tone sounds a bit uncertain, Rebecca. Afraid I'm going to interfere with you doing your job again today?"

That was the last thing she was afraid of.

"Actually, I had something I wanted to do outside the hotel. I thought I'd make sure that you didn't need me this morning, though, before I go."

"No activities planned this morning. I'm glad to see you're getting out."

"Me, too," she said with a smile. "Only, I'm afraid it isn't as simple as that. I'm—I'm hoping you'll go with me. I seem—that is, I'm sorry, but I seem to have made a tiny commitment on your part. It was presumptuous of me, I know, but when Sally begged, I just couldn't say no."

"You had a woman begging you for my presence somewhere?" Okay, when he looked amused and slightly imperious all at the same time, the man was completely irresistible.

"Hey, don't look like you've never had a woman beg you for something, Logan. It just won't fly."

"I think the more unbelievable part is that you said that you just couldn't say no to this—Sally? Weren't you the woman who once claimed she could say no to anything? Something about wide-eyed, tearful urchins?"

She wrinkled her nose. "Okay, you win. I told Sally I'd ask if you'd come and I really want you to come with me today. Will you, Logan?"

"Anywhere, love," he said softly. "You didn't have to try so hard."

But that was because he didn't know where they were going. When he found out that bit of news, she had the feeling he was going to be feeling a bit less magnanimous.

But the words "a bit less magnanimous" paled in comparison to Logan's reaction when she directed the driver to the Eldora Summerstaff Children's Shelter.

His expression froze, his golden eyes turned to ice and he sat beside her in the limo like a very tall, very broad-shouldered, very immovable mannequin.

"Any particular reason you wanted me to come along?" he asked, his voice as expressionless as she'd ever heard it.

"Yes, of course. Every year the Summerstaff Children's Shelter has a party for the kids. Several times a year, actually, since the kids come and go. We always like to have as many of our volunteers on hand as we can get, but in the summer it's difficult because everyone has already been farmed out working for the cause. We also like to have a few donors around. It puts a human face on things for the children."

He turned to her and gently took her hand. "Rebecca, I know you care about this cause deeply, and I also know that you want to think a lot of good things about me that don't really hold true, but did it occur to you that luring me here this way was pretty devious?"

She looked down at her fingers and bit her lower lip.

"Don't do that. You know that I want you—and I want to be very clearheaded right now."

She looked up immediately right into his eyes. "I wasn't trying to make you want me. Really."

"I know that, but Rebecca love, you could make me want you just by fidgeting with your hair the way you're doing right now."

She stopped fidgeting. "I'm sorry, and yes," she said with a sigh. "Of course I know it was devious to lure you to the shelter without telling you where we were going, but darn it, Logan, it would mean so much for these kids to see living proof that they can make a success of themselves. You *are* living proof, you know.''

And maybe Logan would see that children who had been wounded in ways she didn't want to think about could still survive. Not every child who started their life in hell ended up dying at their parents' hands. Mistakes could be corrected. Wrongs could be righted.

"Maybe I'm not so innocent after all, Logan," she said. "Maybe I'm the wolf this time."

And his smile returned.

"Nice try, Red," he said. But he never did completely relax again. When they got to the shelter, he looked around at their surroundings, the seedy side of Eldora, a small part of town, the look in his eyes told her, he had somehow managed to avoid in all his visits to the region.

"This isn't the safest part of town for an innocent," he remarked, and the strain in his voice was evident.

She raised her chin. "It's where these children live. If they can live here, the rest of us can manage to survive for a few hours." She almost told him that poverty wasn't pretty, the standard answer she might give to someone else making such a comment, but it would be an insult to say such a thing to Logan. He knew all about poverty. He knew a great deal more about its ugliness than she ever would.

She knew the minute they walked in the door that she had made a grave mistake. The pain practically rolled off him, even as he pasted on a smile, said a few kind words when he was asked to, and answered the children who approached him with questions. Haltingly. Carefully.

She wanted to help him, to hold him, but she had come here for a purpose. These children needed her, and she had to be there for them. She circled the room, and she stopped to talk with every child she could find. She gave out hugs. When the time came to give out presents, she worked her way to Logan's side.

"All right," he said when she looked up at him pleadingly. "I'll play the wealthy beneficiary. I'll help you with this," he agreed. "Because it isn't these children's fault that I can't handle this…closeness and it isn't your fault, either. But after this, Rebecca, no more. Money isn't enough. It won't ever be enough, and it's all I have to give. You understand that?"

She nodded sorrowfully. "I do, Logan." She understood that he couldn't open his heart, because so many of these children, for all the goodwill given them, would still end up broken. Some of them couldn't be saved and it would be more than this man could stand to watch another child face harm because of something he might or might not do.

"It's not nearly enough, Rebecca," he said again, but he smiled at the children who marched up to him to get their presents. Children with big, dark eyes. Children who'd learned too much of the world too soon. He spoke to them softly, debated the merits of the two Chicago baseball teams with those who brought up the subject, joked about the movie heroes of the moment to others. He talked of inconsequential things. The children did, too, and she understood the reasons. These kinds of joking surface discussions kept all of them from thinking about the darker parts of their lives. It was a survival tactic and both Logan and these kids apparently knew the rules of the game very well.

When they finally left, she followed him out to the car, waited for the driver to shut her door and circle around to let Logan in. For long minutes Logan just sat there. Silent.

She sat there in silence, too, but her heart was breaking for him with every second that passed.

Finally she reached out and touched his hand.

He jerked like a wooden puppet.

"I'm—sorry," she said. "It was presumptuous of me to bring you here, to practice my amateur psychology. I don't think I really understood what you were feeling until now. I probably still don't really understand, but I know enough to know that this was wrong."

Finally he turned to her, his golden eyes haunted. "Don't make the mistake of feeling sorry for me, Rebecca," he said in a voice that was stiff and angry. "Feel sorry for those children. They're the ones who need your concern. I made my escape years ago and the life I lead now is very rich and full and exactly the way I want it. My childhood is ancient history. It's long gone."

But she had a feeling, staring into the depths of his pained golden eyes, that it would never be gone completely. And she could never do anything to change that. Trying would only bring pain to this good, kind and caring man.

She wouldn't try again.

What she would do, Rebecca thought, as they drove back to the hotel, was solidify her escape plans. Get on with making a life after Logan. Soon enough they'd part ways and she had a very strong feeling that she would need to keep herself very busy if she was going to survive those first few weeks. Because as frightening as it was to admit it, she was beginning to understand what kind of pain and regret her former husband had to have felt. She was beginning to care way too much about a man who would never be able to return those feelings. Without even trying to or wanting to, Logan Brewster was stealing her heart, bit by bit, and there was nothing either of them could do to stop the process.

The grand ballroom of the hotel was decorated in shimmering white, deepest rose and silver, but Logan's mind was far from the decor. Neither was he paying much attention to the theatrical production on the stage that Rebecca had arranged. And it wasn't because the performers weren't talented. The audience certainly seemed to be enjoying themselves just fine. It was simply that he was thinking too much about the lady herself.

He knew very well that Rebecca had taken him to that children's shelter today because she was a good woman who wanted to save him from himself. The same way she wanted to save her little friend Jack. The same way she would probably save anyone that she feared was headed for destruction.

She didn't understand that he had already been saved, that he was really very content with his life and all that he had made of it. He loved traveling, never settling down, never staying too long in one place or with one person, and he would cheerfully return to that no-ties life-style—just as soon as he somehow managed to convince the lady of his satisfaction and wipe the worry from her eyes.

But he had to do that somehow. Because—because he did not want to leave here worrying about whether he had left a trace of sadness in her eyes when he left. That would be a crime. It would be...unforgivable.

When intermission rolled around and the guests turned back to their tables and their conversations, he smiled at Rebecca.

"You've outdone yourself again," he whispered.

She rolled her eyes. "You haven't heard a word of the whole play."

Okay, she probably had him there.

He opened his mouth to apologize, but she shook her head and pressed her fingers over his lips to stop him. "It's fine," she said with a smile. "You were preoccupied, but so was I. How else do you think I knew that you weren't paying attention. My mind was on other things, too."

"Good things?" he asked. He hoped it was true.

She nodded and smiled, her sweet pink lips turning up and tempting him to touch them the way only Rebecca's lips could. The way they always did.

"I think they're good things," she agreed. "I'm sure you'll agree when you hear. I just wanted you to know I had some good news today from the Summerstaff offices. One is that thanks to you and our other donors, Summerstaff has had its most prosperous summer so far. The other is that the summer isn't over. There were so many people wanting to help and to hire people that a number of employers went away without having secured the employees they wanted and needed. So some of us whose jobs were more temporary than the others will be able to go on to other tasks for the rest of the summer."

"Us, meaning you?"

"Yes. I talked to the teacher in charge today. She's found another position for me when I leave here in a few days."

Another position. Another employer. Maybe another man looking at her lips and wanting to kiss her each and every time he looked. Another someone wanting to hear her laughter when he woke up every morning. Another man wanting to lead her to his bed every night.

Somehow, from somewhere, Logan dragged forth a slight encouraging smile.

"So, do you know any details of this job you'll be moving on to?" *After you leave my side.*

"A little. My future employer is a widower with two children."

Just the kind of man she was looking for, he couldn't help thinking. A family man, a man with the children she craved.

"He's taking them on a vacation to a cabin in the North Woods of Wisconsin, and he needs a nanny to accompany them."

"Sounds...intriguing," he said with a smile. "Sounds adventurous."

It sounded way too convenient for a single man to have Rebecca at his beck and call while they were virtually alone in a deserted cabin in a lonely stretch of woods. Logan felt the tension climbing his body. He felt the old familiar need to curl his hands into fists and pound out his frustration on the nearest hard surface.

"Have you ever stayed in a cabin, love?" he asked. "Have you?"

He'd stayed in places that were a lot worse than any cabin could be.

"No."

"It's been a long time, but my parents used to take me," she said with a small shrug. "And I figure that anything I've forgotten, I can learn. Like how to make a campfire and hike and fish and roast marshmallows and swim in the lake."

And maybe she could learn to love her widower and he could learn to love her back and they could raise those two children together and make babies, and Rebecca could finally find her happiness. She could have exactly what she'd always wanted.

He should be happy for her. Damn it, he had to be happy for her. She was looking up at him with his favorite look, her violet eyes wide and trusting, her lips soft and yielding.

In that moment, he didn't care that the whole room was there, that they were in full view of his guests. He bent over her and took his kiss. He savored the last lingering taste of her. He might never have a chance to be this close to her again.

"Be happy, love," he said softly. "I'm glad you've found work that can bring you joy."

And he was. But that didn't mean he wasn't dying inside as well.

Chapter Ten

Rebecca's fingers were like frozen twigs as she slid up the zipper on the short silver gown she was wearing to the last major event of Logan's grand opening ceremonies.

The world was spinning away without her, or so it seemed. Only a few days earlier, Emily and Simon had finally declared their hearts to each other. And just the morning before, she and Emily had helped Gideon set the stage as he placed his love on the line for Caroline. Her friends had found the kind of happiness that neither of them had ever thought to find, and she was ecstatic for them. They were her sisters in every way but blood.

But…her own world was more than a little edgy, more than a little frayed, and way beyond painfully confused right now. She was leaving Logan in one more day. As soon as the last straggling guests from this first group departed, she and Logan were going their own ways. And while their paths just might

cross once or twice in the years to come, the chances
of even that happening were slim. Logan had hotels
all over the world and he was always opening new
ones. In the future, other assistants would help him.
Other women would feel the strong press of need
every time he smiled down into their eyes. Other
women he might laugh with and smile at—and take
into his arms.

"Stop it. Don't be this way, Linden," she begged
herself. Wasn't she moving on to good things? She
was. Maybe she'd become friends with her new employer. Maybe he'd want a new wife to mother his
children. Maybe a contented future was waiting for
her just a short distance away, somewhere in the
woods in a small cabin.

But Logan wouldn't be there. She'd never live
these days again, never feel this glow again. Surely
this kind of urgent, desperate longing didn't seek a
woman out more than once in her life.

Please don't let it ever happen to her again. This
time was difficult enough. She was close to tears already.

"And that just won't do," she whispered. "Tonight you have to smile for him, be there for him.
Tonight is the night all his guests will remember the
most. The last magical night." This would be the
night for setting the stage for the Oaks for the weeks
to come. It had to be special. It had to be...perfect.

She kissed her fingers and touched her lips. "I'll
make it perfect for you, Logan," she said with a small
smile. "It's my final gift to you, all that I can do
now."

The cocktail party was progressing nicely, Logan
thought, watching his guests swirl from one group to

another, courted by attentive waiters offering them
some of Jarvis's most excellent fare. The wine was
exquisite and plentiful, the soft strains of Handel's
Water Music floated on the air, and the guests were
clad in their best clothes and their easiest smiles.

There was absolutely no reason he should be feeling so irritable this evening. And yet...he did feel
irritable. Beyond irritable. Abrasive might not be going too far.

He knew the reason why. It was the damned lovely
sprite in silver and diamonds smiling her way through
the crowd. She sparkled, she glowed. Her gentle
laughter wafted to him no matter where he stood. She
was the hit of the party, having a wonderful time en-
tertaining and being entertained while he was a veritable grouch.

Didn't the innocent know that every man in the
room was following her with eyes that simmered with
desire? Didn't she know that he was fully the worst
of the lot? Wasn't she feeling the tiniest bit of regret
that tomorrow she was going to pack her bags and
walk out of his life forever? To some cabin in the
woods. To some other man. One who could give her
what he couldn't. Babies. And love.

"Careful, Brewster," he muttered to himself as he
waved away a glass of wine and strolled over to make
himself pleasant to a throng of businessmen. The lady
had done her job and done it better than he ever could
have dreamed. She had done everything he had asked
and more. It wasn't Rebecca's fault that she had
crawled under his skin and started him thinking about
things that weren't really possible. She owed him
nothing. And considering that he had nothing to offer

her, he should be glad that she would have no trouble sailing out of his life. He should be enjoying his last moments with her. While he still could.

He bid his crowd of businessmen good evening and made his way to the lady's side.

"Jarvis outdid himself tonight," she said.

"*You* outdid yourself tonight," he reminded her.

"And you, too. You dressed me like a princess," she said, glancing down at her silver dress and shoes.

He waved one hand in dismissal. "The dress needed the right woman to wear it. Angelique would have howled if she'd had to put it on anyone else."

Rebecca chuckled. "You made that up."

He gave her a mock frown. "She told me so herself. 'Logan, mon cher,' she said to me, 'I want this dress for Becka and no other woman. You *must* convince her to wear ma creation,'" he said, holding one hand over his heart, just the way the lady in question would have.

"Logan," Rebecca admonished, trying to hide her smile. "Be serious."

"I'm being very serious, love," he said, taking her hand. "Truly serious. Angelique likes you. A lot. You've given her pleasure. You give so many people pleasure. That's important. Don't ever go thinking that we're just playing dress-up with you, love. You have a beautiful soul and are a very beautiful person. And I thank you…for sharing these past few weeks with me."

No way would he insult her by implying what she had done was a mere job. She'd gone way beyond the demands of any job. She'd given him all her time, all her creativity, all her beauty, both inside and out. He was going to miss that, all of it, all of her. That had to be why he felt like his soul was splitting in two.

"They've been…good weeks, haven't they, Logan?" Rebecca looked up into Logan's eyes. She'd been trying so very hard to keep things light, keep things simple, to keep herself from caring—or thinking about the fact that the clock's hands were moving forward, ever forward. Driving her away from him in such a very short time.

"The very best," he assured her. "I'm—I confess I'm going to miss you, sweet lady."

"Me, too," she said softly, trying to keep her tone still somewhat light. Because she would do more than miss him. She would grieve for his loss. But no way did she want him knowing that. He'd feel responsible. He'd worry about her, and what she wanted from him was beyond worry. It was something he couldn't give her, something she didn't want him to know she wanted. He'd called her Red Riding Hood and he must have been right, because she was feeling a bit lost in the woods right now. She was already missing her golden-eyed wolf.

Gently he took her hand. They walked together, traced the halls of the hotel, past the moonlit pool where they'd raced and laughed, past the theater where he'd held her while she cried, and out into the gardens, dark and fragrant with the scent of warm nights and roses, lit only by moonlight and fireflies.

"You'll be leaving tomorrow?" he asked.

She nodded, shivering slightly as his fingers tracked down her arm and found her hand. He brought her hand to his lips and kissed the palm.

"I—yes. I thought I'd say my farewells to everyone this evening since tomorrow people will be busy packing and clearing out.''

He turned her hand over and kissed the back of it, then moved on to each finger.

"And you'll be leaving for Wisconsin—when?" he asked, his voice rough as he murmured against her skin.

Her head was spinning from the nearness of him, the warmth of him, the feel of his lips. The terrible ache of knowing that he was saying goodbye. Right now. Right here. They were ending it.

"I'll be leaving in two days," she said in a choked voice. "I'll be gone for two weeks."

"You've never met this man, Rebecca, have you?"

"No, but Deb has asked a lot of questions. I'll be safe, Logan," she promised. She'd almost called him something else. Love. The word he'd used so many times with her. But with Logan it was a part of his personality, an endearment he dropped easily, just as he was dropping kisses on her fingertips, on the sensitive skin of her wrist. With her, it wouldn't have been that way. She would have meant it. He would have known.

"Be careful, sweet," he said gently. "I'll worry."

He stopped kissing her wrist. He tugged gently and pulled her right into his arms, up close to his heart. He molded his mouth over her own.

Her arms came up automatically. They found their home. She tried to memorize the feel of him, every line of his body, every sensation of his touch. His lips brushed over hers, then consumed her. Giving. Seeking. Demanding.

Rebecca gave back kiss for kiss. She was right where she wanted to be. Forever, it seemed, in spite of how hard she'd fought not to be a fool and fall for Logan. She couldn't stay. If he touched her one more time, if she burrowed any closer into his embrace, she would not be able to hold back any longer. Her secrets would come spilling from her lips. She would ruin this last perfect moment with the last man on earth she'd ever want to hurt or to cause any regret.

She took a deep breath, flattened her palms against the hard warmth of his chest and pushed back. She dragged her lips from his.

"I'd—better go," she somehow managed to say.

He stared at her for long seconds, strain evident in his eyes even in the semidarkness. For just one second she thought he would pull her back to him. And she wanted him to. Desperately wanted him to.

But he opened his arms. He stepped back, took a deep breath. Finally, he smiled. Such a slight smile, but a smile nevertheless.

"Go get 'em, Red. You're like no other woman I've ever met. I'll remember you on nights like this one. It's been—a definite pleasure knowing you. You've given me more than you can know."

He tilted his head in farewell.

"Goodbye, Logan," she whispered.

There was a restlessness inside him after Rebecca left for the night, a howling, haunting need growing within him, and Logan knew that he would never sleep this night. He stood there for five full minutes in the rose garden, the longing for something he'd given up ever having eons ago washing over him. His need for Rebecca was fierce, pulsing, a hunger that he knew was as real as any physical hunger he'd ever had.

The pain was raw. He wouldn't be able to forget her here, not here where he'd held her only moments before. Not ever here. There was only one place to go, a place where a man had to keep his wits about him every minute or risk losing what little he had. Out on the streets where every man, woman and child owned a demon or two.

He needed action, movement, a place where everything was reduced to the lowest common denominators. Want, need, survival. That was where he was tonight. In a place he hadn't been for many long years. A howling animal who'd lost the woman he wanted for his own.

It would be a long night. He might put miles on the soles of his shoes.

"But it won't be enough, Brewster," he whispered, knowing it was true. He might walk and walk. He might get into a brawl, do his best to drown his pain in the meaningless actions people took to forget their troubles.

But in the morning, he would finally have to face reality.

She was going. And he was the fool who was going to let her walk away. It was possibly the best, most generous thing he would ever do in his life.

And someday, when he ran into the lady on the street with her five children and her cabin-loving husband, he'd catch a smile on her face, and maybe he'd feel good about all the things he hadn't said to her today. All the opportunities he'd allowed to pass.

But for now?

"Time to head for your old stomping grounds, buddy." It didn't matter that this was a different town and a different time. On the poor side of town, every day, every time, every town was the same. Desperate and scared. Angry and lonely. He would fit right in tonight.

It was barely dawn but Rebecca was already up and about. Maybe because she hadn't really slept the night before.

This was the day she was to leave and she was hoping that most of the guests would be up and leaving in a few short hours. She longed to make her way to the limo that would carry her away from the Oaks and from Logan. She wanted to get it over with. Without thinking, without giving herself time to hesitate or feel.

Rebecca was doing her darnedest to look natural. She didn't want the few people making their way down to the lobby to see that her smile was as plastic as the credit card in her purse. She waved to someone who called to her, said a quick goodbye, but her ultimate goal for this day was always the door. Escape. The road to forgetfulness.

In a few hours all of this would be over. She was nearly there, well on the way to being able to leave through the big glass-and-oak doors that she'd once so admired, when a woman pushed those very doors open and stepped inside.

The lady was a stranger, not one of the guests who had become so familiar to Rebecca. And yet there was something about her that reminded Rebecca of someone. That shining long brunette mane, the sea-blue eyes, the long model's legs. Pure elegance clad in designer clothing. Born-to-the-manor breeding. Intelligence in that exotic gaze. A smile that could dazzle even a certifiable grouch. No need to train this woman or to change this woman. Any fool could see that she was the perfect match in every way for a man like Logan.

Moving toward Rebecca, the woman held out one slim hand.

"Hi, I'm looking for Logan Brewster. Are you a guest here? Would you know if he's around?"

Rebecca signaled to the desk attendant. She asked him to see if he could page Logan even though it was still awfully early. She didn't really want to call him, but clearly something had happened. Something was up, she thought as she looked at the woman. Taking a deep breath, she took the lady's hand.

"Hello, I'm Rebecca Linden, and no, I'm not a guest. I'm an employee. You must be Allison Myer. I'll have someone ring for Logan if you don't mind waiting."

The woman raised one slim shoulder in an elegant shrug. She held out delicate hands with perfectly polished nails and rings of gold on most of her fingers.

"Logan's worth waiting for, isn't he? And if you don't mind, could you have someone give him a message?"

Rebecca looked up, waiting for the woman to continue.

"Tell him I hope he'll see me and that I'm sorry," the woman said in a voice that could have charmed two-headed dragons.

When Rebecca simply nodded, the woman smiled and shook her head. "We were on the verge of getting engaged, you know, when I left. People said we were the perfect couple."

Rebecca felt like she was trying to swim through

gelatin. She wanted to get away, but she just couldn't move.

"And now you're back."

"Yes," the woman agreed with a pretty smile. "I'm back."

Chapter Eleven

Logan was apparently not answering his page. Rebecca had no choice but to invite Allison into the dining room to have some coffee and to wait.

The woman automatically kicked her shoes off and coiled her legs beneath her, making herself at home. On some women the move might have looked childish or out of place in such elegant surroundings. On Allison, it looked just right.

Allison tilted her head, resting her cheek in the palm of her hand. "You were my replacement, weren't you?"

Rebecca took a deep breath. She sat up straighter. "I was hired to assist Logan for the opening, yes."

The lady smiled as if she had a secret that no one else in the world had ever heard. "Then you know how he is. The man quite simply takes a woman's breath away. He makes you want to jump through hoops in a wild attempt to please him."

Rebecca simply stared at Allison. She did not want

to share confidences about Logan with this woman. Her feelings for him were too precious, too private.

The lady giggled. "You didn't think you were the only woman who'd ever felt like that about him, did you?"

Of course she hadn't. What woman would ever be that foolish?

"Anyway," Allison said with a sigh, sipping her coffee when the waiter brought it to her. "I didn't like feeling like that. Logan and I were considering marriage and I, well, darn it, men had always fallen at my feet. They were the ones rushing around trying to please me. Logan considered me a friend, but I knew he didn't think of me as more, even though he was trying to decide if he wanted to marry me. I liked being the one in charge, and I wasn't. Not with Logan. That was why I ran."

Her voice grew more somber on the last words and Rebecca couldn't help it. She knew she was too soft-hearted. She wanted to hate this woman who was so perfect for Logan, but she just couldn't. Because Allison knew how impossible loving Logan was.

"You should have stayed," she said gently.

"I know. It was wrong to leave him in the lurch when I knew how much this hotel meant to Logan. And it was especially wrong to leave without telling him the exact reason I was going. I just—when Edwin invited me to go with him, and I knew that he was fascinated with me—I just jumped. He seemed so easy compared to Logan. So I left Logan a note telling him I was leaving him for a man with more money, and left Logan and the Oaks behind."

A sharp sense of anger swirled inside Rebecca. She

understood what Allison must have felt, but surely the woman owed Logan more loyalty than that.

"So why did you come back now?" she asked.

Allison shrugged. "To be honest with him the way I should have in the first place. It's occurred to me in these past few weeks that one of the greatest gifts a person can give to another is honesty. Logan and I were close once. I need to apologize to him. More than that, I need to see him."

Rebecca nodded. She tried to ignore the growing pain welling up inside her. No way did she want to be here when Allison and Logan reconciled. She needed to be gone.

Bowing to the lady's wishes to have some alone time to gather her courage for this meeting with Logan, Rebecca realized that she couldn't leave just yet.

Because the woman was right.

Rebecca slowly walked through the corridors of the hotel. She pushed open the door of the theater where she'd had to confess to Logan the truth about her tears. She remembered how they'd touched and laughed. She'd been honest with him that day in a very small, insignificant way.

But like Allison, if she left this hotel today as she'd intended to, without another word between herself and Logan, she would be running from the truth. And she'd already walked that road. Her marriage to James, after all, had been more of a running away from her aunt and uncle rather than a running to the man. She'd never really even explained her feelings to her aunt and uncle. She'd assumed they knew how she felt, but maybe they hadn't. She'd left without giving herself or them a chance to air their feelings.

And isn't that what she was preparing to do with

Logan? Just leave, without even telling him how much she cared, that he'd changed her world?

She sucked in her breath. "He's worth any risk. And I'll make sure he understands completely that I'll be okay even though he doesn't feel the same."

Even though she might never be completely okay for a very long time. Someday she'd be a better, happier person just because she'd known Logan Brewster for a few short weeks.

He should definitely be made aware of that.

The light was just beginning to filter into the streets on the east side of Eldora, and Logan's legs were finally beginning to give out. He'd been walking for hours, trying to walk Rebecca right out of his system.

Because he had to. She was a woman who was warm and giving. A home fires sort of woman who wanted the whole husband and babies and happily ever after dream. How could he ever be the right man for a woman like that? He couldn't. Just look at this part of town, the poverty, the anger, the hurts so deep that nothing could ever heal them. He'd come from a place just like this one, and living this way made a person hard, cold. A man who survived this part of town did so by learning how *not* to feel, not to care, not to love.

He'd learned the lesson so well. Too well. And that was why he absolutely couldn't have this woman he wanted so much. Because she deserved every good thing she wanted. All the trimmings of life. The babies. The devoted father to those babies. A man who felt free to open his heart to the risks of caring.

"You'd be cheating her, Brewster. Depriving her of all the things she needs the most."

But as he continued to roam the streets, as the light began to grow, he couldn't help trying to hold on to Rebecca for a bit longer. He did his best to hold her in his mind.

"What do you think she'd think of this part of town, Brewster?" he asked cynically.

He asked that as if she'd never been to this part of town, but he knew that wasn't so. Her children's shelter was here somewhere. She came here often. She knew what this world was like as much as anyone could who'd never actually lived here.

"And what does she think?" he muttered, looking around him, trying to envision this world through Rebecca-like eyes.

His mind refused to work at first. He saw only what he'd always seen. The dirt, the poverty, the peeling paint on the buildings. All the things that had driven him from a place very much like this and made him determined to get out, to succeed at any cost. To never come back or open his eyes to things that could hurt him again. Like false hope or impossible dreams—or love.

The pain nearly doubled him over, the fact that he was so emotionally lacking that he couldn't even open himself enough to see what was in Rebecca's heart and mind when she walked down a street.

But then he closed his eyes, just for a second, and concentrated with all his will and all his might. He wanted a piece of her for just a moment longer in the only way he could really have her. He tried just a bit harder.

When he opened his eyes, he saw…other things. A young couple walking hand in hand down the street. Smiling in spite of their surroundings. Stopping to wrap their arms about each other, to exchange a kiss or two or three and then walk on, hand in hand again. As if they were really happy. As if dreams could really come true in this place.

He looked again and he saw a mother and a father pushing a baby in a slightly crooked stroller. The husband gestured to the wife to bring her attention to the child, and together they gazed down at the gurgling baby cooing back at them. With his heart in his eyes, the big man dressed all in scuffed leather and torn black denim gently reached for his son. He cuddled the baby close and kissed his forehead. He smiled at the woman who leaned forward and kissed both her husband and her child.

The paint on the buildings seemed a little bit whiter, a little cleaner.

A building could be painted, Logan thought.

"Or at least that's what Rebecca would think," he murmured.

Then he looked at the couple with the child again. He wondered if there had been such couples in his own neighborhood when he was growing up. Maybe there had been. Maybe he just hadn't been able to see. Maybe his hurts had gone so deep that he *couldn't* see or bear to see the hope and happiness of others.

"Don't fool yourself, Brewster. This place needs work and a lot more than hope," he whispered. "There are lost souls who live here."

"You talking to yourself, mister? Don't look like a man who would be talking to himself."

The small voice came from behind him. Logan turned and stared down at a four-foot urchin with a wise grin on his face. The young boy was shaking his head.

Logan grinned. He shrugged sheepishly. "I was just thinking out loud. Do you know the children's shelter down the street?"

The boy looked slightly suspicious, but he nodded. "Sure do. Got this baseball there," he said, tossing the ball into the air. "And this shirt." He tugged on the tail of his shirt so that Logan could see the garment better. "What about it?"

"Do you know the ladies who work there?"

Suspicion turned into a frown. "You got some problem with them? Because if you do, you've got a problem with me, too, mister. Those ladies are my angels. We don't let nothin' hurt them, not even some rich dude like you."

"Then we're agreed," Logan said. "I happen to have a thing about those angels, too. I was just wondering if you felt their shelter had helped you in any way."

The kid gave Logan an exasperated look. "Got a new baseball, don't I? Got a new shirt. The angels are good to us." The indignant look on the child's face grew. "I'm not so sure you know our angels or you wouldn't even be asking dumb questions like that."

And that was how Logan knew that the boy had received more than a shirt and a baseball. Loyalty like that didn't come from simple charity, the donation of funds and gifts. This boy had obviously come face-to-face with something much deeper and stronger. He'd gotten a shot of dignity and caring along with his gifts—and it showed.

He looked down at the boy again and nodded a

salute. "Take care of those angels, then. They're pretty special."

The boy smiled back.

Logan waved goodbye. He walked down the street and he realized he really had been looking at the world through Rebecca's eyes. Because the dirt was still there. Somewhere close by, there was still fear and poverty and even ugliness. Maybe a great deal of ugliness. He'd been one of the lucky ones who had escaped his own ugly neighborhood, but...what if he had to live in a place like this again? What if this place were still his home?

The answer flowed to him like water slipping downstream. He'd want someone who could see the few bright spots at his side. If he lived here, he'd want to live with someone who could make a little hope. Someone loving and caring. One someone.

He wanted that someone very badly right now.

But he couldn't just leave now that he'd gotten what he'd come for. Rebecca would never go without leaving something good behind. When he'd been young, he hadn't been able to change anything. He hadn't been able to help his friend. But he was no longer a kid, and he'd seen a little piece of the world through a warm, caring woman's eyes this time. If she were here, she would do what she *could* do, but instead *he* was the one here today. So he searched the eyes of those on the street for the ones filled with the least amount of hope. A woman whose baby was crying pitifully. A woman who looked much older than she probably was.

He carefully approached her, tentatively smiled down into the baby's tiny face and tucked a bill into the woman's pocket. "Please. It's nothing," he told her when she tried to back away. "I'm sorry for scaring you. Please take the money for the baby," he said, motioning toward the child. "Even though it's not enough. Not nearly enough." And it wasn't. He wanted to give so much more than money, but for now, for this tiny moment, money was what he could give.

Then he walked away. He smiled at every child that he met, said hello to every adult who would meet his eyes, even those who looked nervous and darted away afterward. And he made himself a promise.

"To offer a little hope to some. Whatever I can." Heaven knew that as he made his way back to the hotel and the woman who might already be on her way out of his life, he needed a bit of hope for himself.

He wondered how he was going to break the news to her, that her wolf wanted her overwhelmingly and forever.

Rebecca was pacing the floor, twisting her fingers tightly together by the time the word came through that Logan had returned to the Oaks.

She marched to the lobby, determined to find a private place and tell him the speech she'd started to memorize, the words that would reveal her heart and probably win his pity.

She winced at the thought. But still she kept walking. Only to see Allison linking her arm through his, coaxing him into the depths of the hotel.

Of course. He and Allison had been on the verge of getting married, the woman had said. The lady would have the right to speak to him first, to tell her heart and try to win him back.

For a moment, Rebecca faltered. Maybe she shouldn't say anything at all. Maybe her confession wouldn't reassure Logan, make him feel proud that he had made one woman happy. Maybe he would feel burdened, knowing that she loved him and he couldn't love her back the same way. Perhaps she should just walk away right now.

The coward's way. The easy way.

She shook her head quickly. She settled herself in Logan's office. And waited. Forever, it seemed.

But when the door to Logan's office finally swung back, she realized that she'd only been in there just over ten minutes.

He was smiling. Smiling as if he'd just been given the world's greatest gift.

"I—you saw Allison," she began, her voice coming out as a strained whisper.

He nodded. "Yes. I was surprised to see her again."

Obviously happy he had seen her by the pleased expression on his face. She should get down to business, say what she had to say and then leave. She really, really had to leave, Rebecca thought, seeing that heartbreaking smile transform Logan's handsome face. Those golden eyes were killing her.

She ducked her head…just slightly. "I—I meant to be gone by now," she began. "I know our contract's ended, but—"

She dared to raise her head, to stare right into those golden eyes that were staring at her as if she were the only person on the face of the earth who really mattered. She wondered how many women had felt that way, how many women had faced this painful moment.

But she couldn't think about that. If she did, she could never say what she meant to say.

"I want to thank you," she said, her voice breaking. "I know we've already said goodbye, but—I never told you—I *want* to tell you just how special this time has been for me. I have a good life, a relatively happy life, and yet—while I was here, I felt things I'd never felt before. Because of you. And I just wanted to let you know…how very wonderful you are."

He took a step toward her.

She scurried back and held out her hand. "Not because I want anything from you, you understand. I just wanted—it's just that—I think a person should be told if they change another person's life. If they make a difference. I wanted you to know that before I left."

She wanted to say more, to repeat the words "thank you" and "goodbye," but her throat was closing up. Logan was blurring before her eyes. She knew that in a moment she would be gone and he would resume his life with the woman who never should have left him in the first place, the woman he'd wanted to marry.

Rebecca turned to go. She stumbled forward a step. Then found her progress stopped by a gentle but commanding touch. A warm hand held her arm.

"You can't go," he said. "Not yet, Rebecca."

That statement cleared her eyes. She opened them wide, staring up at him.

"I, that is, your contract doesn't really end until midnight, sweetheart. If you don't believe me, pull it out. We'll go over it together."

He gently tugged on her arm. He pulled her a touch closer, holding her loosely, staring down at her.

"I have to go," she said. "I want to go. Please." It was all she could do to get the words out. She couldn't stay here and work while he reacquainted himself with the woman he was truly meant to have. Not after she'd told him how she felt.

"Rebecca. Love," he said, his own voice breaking. "I'd be willing to tear up that contract, but if we did, we—I'd want to draw up a new one, a different one. If you were willing."

He had moved her into his arms now. She placed her hands out to keep some distance between them, to keep herself from leaning in and touching her lips to his. Her fingers felt the warmth from him, the wild thudding of his heartbeat. She felt the tremor go through his body.

"Logan?"

He reached back onto his desk, pulling out a pen and paper. "Bear with me, love," he whispered, letting go of her to scribble something on the paper. "I have so little experience in this kind of thing. Bear with me. I promise I won't hurt you."

He hastily wrote down a few sentences. He placed the paper in her hands.

She looked down at the ivory vellum, read the words written there and closed her eyes.

He had drawn up a new contract. The terms were simple.

Opening her eyes, she read the words: "I, Logan Brewster, solemnly pledge to love you, Rebecca Linden, forever. In return, you, Rebecca Linden, agree to love me in your own way for as long as you possibly can. Both of us agree to make the world a better place for children, our own, and as many more as we possibly can."

He had signed his name in bold sprawling letters.

She looked up, deep into his eyes, trying to understand, trying desperately not to misunderstand.

"I thought that you and Allison—"

"Were all wrong for each other. She didn't come here to make things up with me, love. She came here to apologize and to assure Edwin, the man she really loves, that she and I have patched our fences and both moved on. That we are, in fact, over and out of each other's systems."

"But you wanted to marry her."

He grinned. "I was considering a business arrangement that would have been a marriage of convenience. That's not what I'll have with you if you'll have me."

"I'm not convenient?"

He shook his head slowly, leaned his hips back against the desk and tumbled her farther into his arms. "Very inconvenient since I think of you when I'm supposed to be working—or eating—or sleeping. And very wonderful, angel. You're the first woman to make me want to stop my wandering."

She knew her eyes were somewhat stricken when she looked up at him this time. She didn't want him to ever resent her in any way or regret bringing her into his life.

"But I wouldn't want you to change your life-style for me, Logan. I—"

He shushed her with two gentle fingers covering her lips.

"My life-style and my position can be very useful in helping others, love. But without you, I'm poverty-stricken. I'm destitute. Money can work miracles, it's true, but love is what matters most in life. Of course, I do understand, angel, that you really don't want someone who's going to demand an everlasting, overwhelming love from you. I'm willing to take whatever you can offer.''

She smiled down at him, played with the buttons on his shirt. "And if I told you that I love you desperately?''

He groaned, covered her hand with his own.

"Don't say it if you don't mean it, Rebecca. Please.''

The pain she'd seen once before glimmered in his eyes. She grasped the front of his shirt and pressed herself close. "I never thought I could love like this, Logan. I would never give you less than all my love.''

He kissed her then. Softly. Gently. But she could feel the urgency simmering beneath the surface.

"And you'll marry me?'' he asked, his beautiful voice thick with emotion.

"Yes. Definitely yes. If you're sure. I know I'm not the kind of woman you ever thought to settle down with.''

He tucked his finger under her chin. His golden eyes glowed with love. "You're what I want, love. Every day. I want you beside me at the first light of day and in my arms in the dark hours of the night. I want you in my heart and in my life always.''

She smiled into his eyes then.

"Is that in the contract, Logan?''

"Absolutely, Red,'' he said, kissing her lips in brief little nips. "It's business, pure and simple.'' He kissed her again.

Rebecca angled her head, returning his kiss with all the love in her heart.

"And is this business, too?" she murmured against his lips.

Logan pulled back slightly and raised one brow. "It's the best kind," he said. "From now on, I'm in the business of loving you. Full time."

And he pulled her close and claimed her for his own.

Epilogue

It was hard to believe that more than a year had passed, Rebecca thought, gazing up at her husband as he stood waiting with her for the ceremonies to begin. Emily had finally opened her school for unwed mothers and today they were having their first official Christmas party. Everyone was here. Emily and Simon, of course, had brought their little son. And Gideon and Caroline were there with the twins. All of them looked especially pleased to be here, but Logan was the only one that Rebecca really saw right now. Standing there, holding their two-year-old daughter, Essie, whom they'd only managed to adopt two weeks before, he was more handsome than she'd ever seen him. He held the little girl in the crook of his arm and whispered to her constantly, smiling down at her as she jabbered back.

Rebecca ran her hand over her still smooth abdomen. Another one on the way and Logan was ecstatic. She was so very lucky to have found this man.

As if her thoughts had sounded in his ear, he turned and gazed down at her.

"Are you feeling all right?" he asked, a trace of worry in his eyes as his gaze traveled to where her hand was still pressed to her stomach.

She grinned. "Just counting my blessings, Logan. There really are a lot of people here today, aren't there?"

He smiled his pleasure at her words. "Yes. Probably because Caroline did an excellent job of publicizing this event to the business community. Everyone wanted to help and to be here to share in this first Christmas. I'm just glad that things have worked out so well."

Rebecca shook her head. "As if you didn't know they would. You've been devoting so much energy to this project, it's amazing your next hotel is even going to open on time. Not that it wouldn't. You always manage to hire people who know how to get things done."

He raised one brow and grinned. "Yes, I do, don't I?"

She wrinkled her nose at him. "Hush. I didn't mean me. I meant, well, you know what I meant. I'm glad you and Edwin hired Allison as manager. I can't believe the two of you went into partnership together on this hotel. You did it just for her, didn't you? Because she adores him, but she still feels a bit of loyalty to old friends."

He shrugged. "I rather like Edwin, you know. Even if he and I usually compete head-to-head. He's good for Allison. Besides, if he hadn't stolen her away, I wouldn't have met you, sweetheart. I hope he and Allison have many wonderful years and make many wonderful children.''

"Like us?''

''No one's like us, love. No other man has you in his bed every night and in his dreams every day.''

Rebecca's heart filled with sunshine at his words. She touched his sleeve and smiled up at him.

Logan pulled his wife off to the side and gathered her close. ''What on earth did a man like me ever do to deserve a woman like you, Rebecca?'' he whispered against her hair.

Rebecca pulled back far enough to stare into the golden eyes she adored so much. ''You went to an auction looking for an employee.''

''And found love instead,'' he agreed with a smile.

''*We* found love, Logan.''

''More than I could ever have hoped for,'' he said, rubbing his hand over her stomach.

''And if there are more?'' she asked.

''Then I'll be the happiest man alive.''

''I thought you were already that,'' she teased.

He smiled down at her. ''I am that. The happiest man.''

''Married to the luckiest woman in the world.''

Logan shook his head. ''You once worried that I'd try to change you into the perfect woman, but you *are* and always were the perfect woman for me, you know,'' he said. ''You always know the right words to make me ache for you in every way.''

''And I know what to do, too,'' she said, rising on her toes and pressing her lips to his, lightly resting her hand on their child.

''You certainly do, my love. You certainly do.'' Her golden wolf drew her closer. He mated his mouth to hers and she melted into his embrace as the other guests looked on, smiling their approval.

"Have I ever told you what a weakness I have for golden-eyed wolves?" she whispered, smiling against his mouth.

She felt his own smile forming over hers. "Tell me, love," Logan whispered as Rebecca leaned close and gave him what he wanted.

And later that night, in their moonlit bed, he took her into his arms, placed his lips over hers, and thanked her as only her very own wolf, her heart, her love could ever do.

* * * * *

COMING NEXT MONTH

#1456 FALLING FOR GRACE—Stella Bagwell
An Older Man

The moment Jack Barrett saw his neighbor, he wanted to know everything about her. Soon he learned beautiful Grace Holliday was pregnant and alone…and too young for him. He also found out she needed protection—from *his* jaded heart….

#1457 THE BORROWED GROOM—Judy Christenberry
The Circle K Sisters

One thing held Melissa Kennedy from her dream of running a foster home—she was single. Luckily, her sexy ranch foreman, Rob Hanson, was willing to be her counterfeit fiancé, but could Melissa keep her borrowed groom…forever?

#1458 DENIM & DIAMOND—Moyra Tarling

Kyle Masters was shocked when old friend Piper Diamond asked him to marry her. He wasn't looking for a wife, yet how could he refuse when without him, she could lose custody of her unborn child? It also didn't hurt that she was a stunning beauty….

#1459 THE MONARCH'S SON—Valerie Parv
The Carramer Crown

One minute she'd washed ashore at the feet of a prince, the next, commoner Allie Carter found herself "companion" to Lorne de Marigny's son…and falling for the brooding monarch. He claimed his heart was off-limits, yet his kisses suggested something else!

#1460 JODIE'S MAIL-ORDER MAN—Julianna Morris
Bridal Fever!

Jodie Richards was sick of seeking Mr. Right, so she decided to marry her trustworthy pen pal. But when she went to meet him, she found his brother, Donovan Masters, in his place. And with one kiss, her plan for a passionless union was in danger….

#1461 LASSOED!—Martha Shields

Pose as a model for a cologne ad? That was the *last* job champion bull-rider Tucker Reeves wanted. That is, until a bull knocked him out…and Tucker woke up to lovely photographer Cassie Burch. Could she lasso this cowboy's hardened heart for good?

Look Who's Celebrating Our 20th Anniversary:

"Happy 20th birthday, Silhouette. You made the writing dream of hundreds of women a reality. You enabled us to give [women] the stories [they] wanted to read and helped us teach [them] about the power of love."

—*New York Times* bestselling author
Debbie Macomber

"I wish you continued success, Silhouette Books.... Thank you for giving me a chance to do what I love best in all the world."

—International bestselling author
Diana Palmer

"A visit to Silhouette is a guaranteed happy ending, a chance to touch magic for a little while.... It refreshes and revitalizes and makes us feel better.... I hope Silhouette goes on forever."

—Award-winning bestselling author
Marie Ferrarella

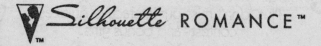

Silhouette ROMANCE™

SILHOUETTE'S 20ᵀᴴ ANNIVERSARY CONTEST
OFFICIAL RULES
NO PURCHASE NECESSARY TO ENTER

1. To enter, follow directions published in the offer to which you are responding. Contest begins 1/1/00 and ends on 8/24/00 (the "Promotion Period"). Method of entry may vary. Mailed entries must be postmarked by 8/24/00, and received by 8/31/00.

2. During the Promotion Period, the Contest may be presented via the Internet. Entry via the Internet may be restricted to residents of certain geographic areas that are disclosed on the Web site. To enter via the Internet, if you are a resident of a geographic area in which Internet entry is permissible, follow the directions displayed on-line, including typing your essay of 100 words or fewer telling us "Where In The World Your Love Will Come Alive." On-line entries must be received by 11:59 p.m. Eastern Standard time on 8/24/00. Limit one e-mail entry per person, household and e-mail address per day, per presentation. If you are a resident of a geographic area in which entry via the Internet is permissible, you may, in lieu of submitting an entry on-line, enter by mail, by hand-printing your name, address, telephone number and contest number/name on an 8"x 11" plain piece of paper and telling us in 100 words or fewer "Where In The World Your Love Will Come Alive," and mailing via first-class mail to: Silhouette 20ᵗʰ Anniversary Contest, (in the U.S.) P.O. Box 9069, Buffalo, NY 14269-9069; (In Canada) P.O. Box 637, Fort Erie, Ontario, Canada L2A 5X3. Limit one 8"x 11" mailed entry per person, household and e-mail address per day. On-line and/or 8"x 11" mailed entries received from persons residing in geographic areas in which Internet entry is not permissible will be disqualified. No liability is assumed for lost, late, incomplete, inaccurate, nondelivered or misdirected mail, or misdirected e-mail, for technical, hardware or software failures of any kind, lost or unavailable network connection, or failed, incomplete, garbled or delayed computer transmission or any human error which may occur in the receipt or processing of the entries in the contest.

3. Essays will be judged by a panel of members of the Silhouette editorial and marketing staff based on the following criteria:

> Sincerity (believability, credibility)—50%
> Originality (freshness, creativity)—30%
> Aptness (appropriateness to contest ideas)—20%

Purchase or acceptance of a product offer does not improve your chances of winning. In the event of a tie, duplicate prizes will be awarded.

4. All entries become the property of Harlequin Enterprises Ltd., and will not be returned. Winner will be determined no later than 10/31/00 and will be notified by mail. Grand Prize winner will be required to sign and return Affidavit of Eligibility within 15 days of receipt of notification. Noncompliance within the time period may result in disqualification and an alternative winner may be selected. All municipal, provincial, federal, state and local laws and regulations apply. Contest open only to residents of the U.S. and Canada who are 18 years of age or older, and is void wherever prohibited by law. Internet entry is restricted solely to residents of those geographical areas in which Internet entry is permissible. Employees of Torstar Corp., their affiliates, agents and members of their immediate families are not eligible. Taxes on the prizes are the sole responsibility of winners. Entry and acceptance of any prize offered constitutes permission to use winner's name, photograph or other likeness for the purposes of advertising, trade and promotion on behalf of Torstar Corp. without further compensation to the winner, unless prohibited by law. Torstar Corp and D.L. Blair, Inc., their parents, affiliates and subsidiaries, are not responsible for errors in printing or electronic presentation of contest or entries. In the event of printing or other errors which may result in unintended value multiples or duplication of prizes, all affected contest materials or entries shall be null and void. If for any reason the Internet portion of the contest is not capable of running as planned, including infection by computer virus, bugs, tampering, unauthorized intervention, fraud, technical failures, or any other causes beyond the control of Torstar Corp. which corrupt or affect the administration, secrecy, fairness, integrity or proper conduct of the contest, Torstar Corp. reserves the right, at its sole discretion, to disqualify any individual who tampers with the entry process and to cancel, terminate, modify or suspend the contest or the Internet portion thereof. In the event of a dispute regarding an on-line entry, the entry will be deemed submitted by the authorized holder of the e-mail account submitted at the time of entry. Authorized account holder is defined as the natural person who is assigned to an e-mail address by an Internet access provider, on-line service provider or other organization that is responsible for arranging e-mail address for the domain associated with the submitted e-mail address.

5. Prizes: Grand Prize—a $10,000 vacation to anywhere in the world. Travelers (at least one must be 18 years of age or older) or parent or guardian if one traveler is a minor, must sign and return a Release of Liability prior to departure. Travel must be completed by December 31, 2001, and is subject to space and accommodations availability. Two hundred (200) Second Prizes—a two-book limited edition autographed collector set from one of the Silhouette Anniversary authors: Nora Roberts, Diana Palmer, Linda Howard or Annette Broadrick (value $10.00 each set). All prizes are valued in U.S. dollars.

6. For a list of winners (available after 10/31/00), send a self-addressed, stamped envelope to: Harlequin Silhouette 20ᵗʰ Anniversary Winners, P.O. Box 4200, Blair, NE 68009-4200.

Contest sponsored by Torstar Corp., P.O. Box 9042, Buffalo, NY 14269-9042.

PS20RULES

ENTER FOR
A CHANCE TO WIN*

Silhouette's 20th Anniversary Contest

Tell Us Where in the World
You Would Like *Your* Love To Come Alive...
And We'll Send the Lucky Winner There!

Silhouette wants to take you wherever
your happy ending can come true.

Here's how to enter: Tell us, in 100 words or less,
where you want to go to make your love come alive!

In addition to the grand prize, there will be 200
runner-up prizes, collector's-edition book sets
autographed by one of the Silhouette anniversary
authors: **Nora Roberts, Diana Palmer,
Linda Howard** or **Annette Broadrick**.

DON'T MISS YOUR CHANCE TO WIN!
ENTER NOW! No Purchase Necessary

Where love comes alive™

Visit Silhouette at www.eHarlequin.com to enter, starting this summer.

Name: _____

Address: _____

City: _____ State/Province: _____

Zip/Postal Code: _____

Mail to Harlequin Books: **In the U.S.:** P.O. Box 9069, Buffalo, NY
14269-9069; **In Canada:** P.O. Box 637, Fort Erie, Ontario, L4A 5X3

*No purchase necessary—for contest details send a self-addressed stamped envelope to:
Silhouette's 20th Anniversary Contest, P.O. Box 9069, Buffalo, NY, 14269-9069 (include
contest name on self-addressed envelope). Residents of Washington and Vermont may
omit postage. Open to Cdn. (excluding Quebec) and U.S. residents who are 18 or over.
Void where prohibited. Contest ends August 31, 2000.

PS20CON_R2